En——

in

Paris

By Jenny O'Brien

By Jenny O'Brien

Ideal Girl Trilogy
Ideal Girl
Girl Descending
Unhappy Ever After Girl

Englishwoman in Trilogy
Englishwoman in Paris
Englishwoman in Scotland
Englishwoman in Manhattan

Englishman in Blackpool, free prequel

For children
Boy Brainy

Short Story
Dunkirk – Rescuing Robert

Praise for Jenny O'Brien

"I absolutely adored this story. It was fun, flirty, romantic, tragic, emotionally heart-breaking at times but also very heart-warming." Adele for "Kraftireader" book blog.

"Jenny O"Brien did a great job creating a story that will let you go through all sorts of emotions. You will laugh and be shocked but you will also feel the love." Anniek for "With love for books" book blog.

"Another wonderful, romantic cosy read beautifully written with warmth love and tenderness." Michele Turner.

"She captures the reader from the first paragraph, engrossing them with her heroine"s journey of love and loss, to the very end." Susan Godenzi, writer.

Acknowledgements

First, thanks most go the builder that inspired this little book. I don't know his name, or indeed anything about him. In fact, I was writing a very different book when I spotted him swinging off the outside of next door's extension and had that lightbulb moment.

Thank you, Beverley Ann Hopper for all your support and for allowing me to borrow your name, I used it gently!

Thanks also to Simon Cruickshank for letting me include the amazing Ship Inn at Stonehaven; a special place.

Finally, thanks as always to my ever supportive family for putting up with all the new characters I keep introducing. At least they're only on paper and don't hog the bathroom.

To Maria Claire

"Wounded by the dart of love."

King Henry V111 to Anne Boleyn, 1527.

Chapter One

6th May. I still don't have a date for the weekend. I've bought the frock, and the most delightful six inch pale grey stilettoes with diamante heels. But posh frocks aren't going to appease my parents. I promised them a man. I lied. There is no man and there isn't going to be unless I can conjure one up over the next couple of days. I'm even prepared to pay. Any idea what the going rate is for a fake boyfriend?

""What about him then?"
"Which one?"
"What, there's more than one?"

The Right Honourable Lady Sarah Cosgrave followed the direction of Cara's hand. She didn't need to glance too hard to recognise the familiar sight of the tall stocky builder. She couldn't really miss him, being as he was a good head taller than the other brickies clambering up and down the scaffolding like trapeze artists.

"Mmm, which part of him are you looking at exactly? The only parts of interest to my father are the length of his vowels and the size of his…"

"Prospects?"

They both burst into a fit of giggles at the thought of the Earl spending even one nano-second in the company of the extremely handsome builder.

"So I was right. You have noticed what a scenic part of Paris you live in, and I'm not talking about Le Pont Neuf!" she added, waving a hand toward the oldest bridge on the Seine.

"I'd be blind not to, but just how you think some buff French brickie will help me out of my current difficulty, I can't imagine," her voice dry.

"I can think of many difficulties I'd be more than happy for him to help me out of; my coat, my shoes, my blouse, my skirt, my stockings, my k..."

"Cara!" she exploded, unable to dampen down her laughter.

"Okay Okay, I'll behave myself for once. So your parents are arriving on Friday expecting to meet..."

"My boyfriend." Still smiling, she paused on the edge of the kerb to throw a glance at her balcony and the little window box dripping with bright red geraniums. She let her eyes roam over the other balconies, all similarly decked out with an assortment of flowers and sighed again. It might not be much. It might not be a patch on Cosgrave Manor but it was hers, her smile turning to a frown.

"If I hadn't lied, they'd have thrown Rupert Reynolds–Smythe in my direction again."

"But…"

"But nothing, Cara. My baguette is well and truly baked on that particular score. I hoped they'd be happy to hear I'm dating but not a bit of it. I'll be lucky to get a hug before they launch into a pile of awkward questions, like the state of his bank balance. And I don't even *have* a boyfriend." She threw a final glance across at the building site. "So now I go home and marry Rupert."

"What, that boring stick in the mud who's old enough to be your father? You can't!"

"Cara, I have no choice. It's either Rupert, some other jumped up squirt, or…"

"Or stand up to your parents for once in your life."

"You of all people should realise it's not that easy," she replied, placing her saxophone on the ground. "I come into my inheritance in a few weeks and that photo of me in the newspaper was the last straw."

"But all you were doing was sitting in a café with a…"

"With a coffee and my sax for company, the way I'm happiest. It was the poor little rich girl by-line that had my parents incensed and then, when the offers of marriage started, they lost it completely. Hopper has been beside himself with all the extra recycling it's created. Apparently he's had to make room in one of the outbuildings to store all the additional paper, and as for the bouquets and chocolates… The local florist has been instructed to divert any blooms addressed to me to the local old people's home but the chocolates are another thing." She cradled Cara's hand within hers. "Hopper, between you, me and the gatepost is a chocoholic and, as he said himself in his last text, if it wasn't for the freebee truffles he'd be well on his way to the job agency."

"What, do butlers have to…?"

"No, silly. Hopper is worth his weight in gold, or should that be chocolate, and boy doesn't he make sure we know it."

She leant across to pull her friend into a brief hug before kissing her on both cheeks. "I've had the most amazing year studying music at the Sorbonne, Cara but it's over now. Don't worry; I'll be fine, more than fine," patting her on the back with more assurance than she felt. "I'll see you tomorrow in the canteen."

With drooping shoulders she stood on the edge of the pavement waiting for a gap in the traffic, her mind scrolling over the past.

She was her own worst enemy. She always had been. She'd have thought her parents would have been happy the only thing she was interested in was music, and classical at that. But it seemed not. As soon as the date of her twenty-third birthday loomed, all they were worried about was palming her on to a serious-minded city type. It didn't matter who it was as long as he carried on looking after the family fortune while they carried on doing what they were best at; abdicating any and all parental responsibility.

Unless she could come up with a half decent boyfriend by Friday, her parents would pull the rug out from under her and set Rupert on her like a sprat dangling after a mackerel. She was fed up with running away from the future they were so determined for her to have, a future full of false friends and even falser…

"*Mademoiselle.* Stop!"

She'd heard the shout but thought nothing of it until he'd added the *stop*.

Turning, the question on her lips died as she found herself looking straight at her builder, or to be exact, his chest. He was taller than she'd imagined; taller, broader and sexier although that didn't seem possible. Craning her head her eyes finally touched his and the force of what seemed like a thousand watt light bulb exploded inside her stomach.

She'd thought him handsome before in that cool arrogant way that seemed to be the French trademark. His nose, high-bridged and slightly crooked might be a little too big but it screamed strength and authority. His dark, weather-beaten skin stretched over high cheekbones any model would be proud of. His mouth set, stubborn even but with a sensual bottom lip twitching, just as the corners of his eyes were crinkling up in silent merriment.

The nervous laugh that welled up in the back of her throat at meeting him face to face died as his gaze pinned itself to hers in an hypnotic trance before starting a lazy trail across her skin. A schoolgirl blush raced across her cheeks and she tilted her chin in the only act of defiance available in light of his visual assault. His eyes, now self-assured and possessive lingered for what seemed like an inordinately long time on her mouth.

She lifted her chin even higher her eyes taking in the thick dark texture of his hair and the way it curled over the neck of his t-shirt before replying. The fact she'd spent the last three weeks ogling him from the security of her flat was a secret she intended to keep.

"Monsieur?" She finally managed, her voice clipped in the best representation of hauteur she could muster under the circumstances.

"Mademoiselle, your bag I believe?"

Her eyes rounded as she tried to make sense of his words. Struggling to reinstate control over her muscles was difficult enough and now he expected her to follow an actual conversation with sentences and all?

What bag? She didn't have a bag with her; she didn't even bother with a purse at college, only her phone and a few Euros stuffed in her back pocket. Dragging her eyes away she allowed them travel the brief distance to her saxophone strap dangling from his hand.

Her face, so recently pink, blanched white at the sight of her vintage Selmer, her very expensive reconditioned vintage Selmer. It had been an eighteenth birthday present from her parents and her most treasured possession, a possession she'd abandoned in the middle of the pavement without a thought as she'd gossiped about men and other inconsequential topics.

This proved her parents were right to be worried about her. In fact she might as well admit defeat and marry Rupert. She could pack up the apartment and hitch a lift back with them next week. Her mother would want to visit that little dressmaker on the Rue de

Passy while her father continued sorting out the assaults on his cellars by restocking at the wine merchants along the Rue Daguerre. But, by Monday, they'd be chomping to get back to their Berkshire estate and she should go with them and accept the diamond Rupert assured her he'd been carrying around for months.

She didn't notice his sudden look of alarm, her gaze now fixed on the black faded case.

"*Mademoiselle*," concern causing his delicious French accent to elongate the last syllable with undue resonance.

"Oh, sorry. Thank you, I'm indebted," stretching out her hand to relieve him of his burden, only to find the case now flung across his shoulders as if it was a sack of spuds and not a near priceless musical instrument.

"Thanks again *monsieur*," she repeated. "But I'm perfectly able to carry my own…"

"Pascal."

"Excuse me?"

"Call me Pascal." He smiled down at her. "And you are?"

"And I'm what?"

She was utterly confused that's what she was. One minute she's minding her own business and the next some strange bloke appears out of nowhere and starts interrogating her with the stupidest of questions. It was a bloody cheek that's what it was as she dismissed the weeks she'd spent staring at him from afar.

Checking out the view from the comfort of her own apartment was one thing; having him materialise in the form of one hundred percent man was completely different; different and confusing as her heartbeat ratcheted up a couple of notches. She could cope with the likes of Rupert until the cows came home, but sexy strangers accosting her in the street? There was nothing in her repertoire of relationships to give her even an inkling of how she was meant to respond. She wanted to run across the road to the safety of her apartment and probably would have, except for the saxophone strap still hanging across his shoulders.

"You are called?"

"Oh I see," although she didn't, she didn't see at all.

Her gaze flickered up to his, only to be caught in the rays of his stare. Mad, that's what he was, positively barking. Some mad French builder had hold of her sax and he wouldn't give it back until she told him her first name. She didn't know what to do, but if she didn't tell him, he might make off with the most treasured of her possessions.

"Sarah."

"Ah, Sarah. *Très Belle*."

She blushed again. Whilst far from fluent she could sort of work out he thought her name beautiful although, by the way his gaze barely wavered from her face it wasn't just her name.

"Sarah, would you, er..." His voice stalled, his eyes uncertain. She would have said he was nervous although what a man like him had to be nervous about was beyond her. She'd never met such a good looking specimen, and she'd met quite a few at those charity balls her mother liked to frequent. But all the celebrity footballers, polo players and crown princes couldn't hold a candle to this humble French builder. This humble French builder still in possession of her sax!

"Would you like to go for a coffee?"

"*J'regret*... I have, how do you say - a date?"

The words were automatic, being as she repeated them on almost a daily basis to an array of men keen to spend time in her company. It was easier to fake a boyfriend than have to explain she wasn't born yesterday. There was no boyfriend and there wasn't likely to be with the current media furore over her pending inheritance. Every Smart Alec reporter and eligible male within miles took an undue interest in her private life, which was all the more reason for her to keep it private. So she did what she had to in the circumstances, which was lie. There was no date apart from with a bath and a book but he wasn't to know that. There was no way she'd go anywhere with him, or any other man, no matter how buff they were. She was in need of a decoy for Friday, but a date with him - no.

"*Naturellement.*" He replied with a quirk of his eyebrow. "Another time perhaps." He lifted the saxophone off his back and set it at her feet.

"Well goodbye, and thanks again."

Reaching up a hand, he went to stroke her cheek only to pause millimetres away from her skin before allowing his hand to drop to his side.

"*Au revoir, ma petite.*"

* * *

He couldn't believe how tongue tied he'd been in front of her. A spotty teenager would have done better.

She'd been indebted to him. She'd been so indebted she'd given him the brush off and, the most surprising part was he'd let her. He'd let her turn him down with little more than a gallant Gallic shrug, his mind full of forever unsaid thoughts and words. All he'd wanted was a chance, a chance to spend five minutes in her company. But, apart from running down the street with her case strapped to his back he had little choice other than to hand it back and walk away.

He headed to the building site to pick up his own case, his mind still full of the sight of her and not only the sight. He remembered the slight smell of her perfume; something light and flowery that assailed his senses as he'd handed over her instrument. He hadn't imagined what she'd smell like. He hadn't given a thought to the rest of her; her voice, soft and melodious as she'd struggled with the French pronunciation. He'd have liked to have touched her, his hand caress her pale English skin. But he knew that would be one sensation too many, even for him. He was only a man; a man madly in love with the image of a woman, the image now a reality beyond his fiercest desire.

He'd earmarked her as being different that first morning on site, different in a good way. Parisian women were in a class of their own. He was privy every day to just how chic a true Parisian woman could be and yet he'd never met one who could hold a flicker to her flame.

Was it the way she held her head, or the directness of her gaze? It wasn't her hair because the three weeks he'd known her he'd never seen it other than dragged off her face in a stern ponytail. She had a good body, or at least he imagined it good underneath the layer upon layer of student garb she housed it in. There were the regimented jeans and leggings and an assortment of sloppy shirts and cardigans that no self-respecting French woman would be seen dead in, and then there was her bag: her black bag, which she had glued to her side, day and night. He'd sort of worked out she was a student at the Sorbonne. It was that or busker on the Metro. It didn't really matter what she was. All that mattered was she wasn't his and after their little interlude he didn't think she ever would be.

Making his way into the office he stuffed a pile of papers from the top drawer into his briefcase before shutting it with a sharp click. It was fortuitous she'd refused him because he'd need all his wits about him if tomorrow's meeting was to go to plan.

Turning off the lights, and pulling the door shut he cast a professional eye up at the roof. They'd just about finished the exterior now and with the electricians, plasterers and plumbers arriving tomorrow, it was time to look at the next stage of the project.

Leaving the site, his eyes shifted of their own accord back to her apartment. He felt like a voyeur standing staring up at her window but he couldn't seem to help himself, his eyes snagging on the sight of her sitting on the balcony with a mug in her hands. She didn't look as if she was going out on a hot date. She didn't look as if she had any intention of moving anytime soon. She looked sad, but there was nothing he could do about that at the moment that wouldn't be wrong on all levels.

He made his way off the building site, ensuring the security gate clicked shut behind him. He had more things to worry about than some chit of a girl with a penchant for saying no. Tomorrow he'd find out whether the bank would support his project for a little while longer. But even thoughts of the meeting ahead couldn't dislodge the image of her from his memory or the smell of a summer garden that seemed to have possessed all his senses.

"Bonjour. So who's turn is it today boys?" he said, wondering who they were haranguing as he clambered up to the top of the scaffolding.

Builders were the same the world over; if it was half good-looking and even if it wasn't they wolf-whistled and cat-called like the best of them. The more prosaic would argue until they were blue in the face it was their social duty to help the less attractive of the species feel better about themselves. He'd even heard some argue that because they were offering a free psychoanalyst service, the government should offer them a tax discount. But as project manager he viewed it as part of his role to at least try to moderate their more extreme remarks. But this morning's meeting with the bank had made him late; too late to even have breakfast as he crammed the remains of a croissant into his mouth with one hand while pressing a hard hat to his head with the other.

"God, look at her, she's right up for it."

"Come on boys, that's a bit off now isn't it," he interrupted, joining them to peer over the edge of the roof.

He'd promised himself he'd try to avoid her apartment block. After all it shouldn't be that difficult as she'd have left by now. If he wasn't on site by 7.30 on the dot, he'd miss her licking those last crumbs off her top lip, and that wasn't something he'd miss out of choice any morning. If he had his way, he'd be there joining her.

He followed their gaze more out of interest than anything. The street was starting to calm down with all the yummy mummy's on the school run while the sexy secretaries would be well ensconced behind the Paris Match on the Metro. It was now the turn of the old ladies, their brown wicker shopping baskets loaded with an assortment of goodies from the boulangerie and charcuterie opposite. There was no way his men would shout out to these matriarchs, not if they valued their jobs.

"Come on boss, you must admit those legs are a smasher. She's a tease, that's what she is lying stretched out on her balcony like that with her robe up to her…"

"Who's a tease?" He stumbled as he realised they weren't staring at the road but at the block of apartments opposite, not just any old apartment, her apartment. His heart filled the sudden hollow inside his chest as his eyes fixed on the sight of her lying across her balcony with her robe indeed right up to her thighs.

His eyes shifted across to his men, even though all his attention was still focussed on the apartment; her apartment. She must have fallen, be ill or worse. Thoughts scattered across his mind even as he started shouting out directions.

"Right, back to it you lot. If we all pull our weight we'll be able to work inside from midday and I'll buy you a beer to celebrate," his voice brusque.

"But…?" Five sets of eyes followed him as he vaulted across the scaffolding like an ape before almost catapulting himself down the ladder at break neck speed.

The knocking and shouting were relentless, but finally the sound of her name reverberating and echoing across the room brought her to her senses. Opening her eyes she found herself staring at blue sky even as she registered the hard cold metal of the balcony biting into her bum. Turning her head she fixed her sight on the trailing edge of a geranium head. She'd have some dead heading to do later but not now; now she had more important things to worry about.

Her mind focussed; the relentless thumping pulling her back with a sense of immediacy. Why she was lying on her balcony in her dressing gown was another matter, one she'd have to think about later. First she had to stop the banging before the whole of Paris came out to see what all the commotion was.

Sitting up was a mistake as a wave of nausea washed over her. Instead she rolled on her stomach and crawled into the living room, the ceramic tiles cool against her bare knees. It was more of a drag than a crawl as shooting pains attacked her right ankle with enough force to fill her eyes to overflowing.

Reaching the door took an age, but was all the more rewarding when she finally managed to touch the dark wood before flopping out across the floor. It took another couple of minutes before she could leaver herself up to standing by gripping the frame with clenched fists. Stretching out a cautious hand, she fumbled for the lock, remembering just in time to secure the chain in place.

"Oui?"

"Sarah, it's me."

Oh that's great. Ever the *comics* these Frenchmen! She prised her left eye open to see who was shouting at her, her vision hampered by a sudden pile driving headache. She could barely stand, let alone see through eyes moist with unshed tears and yet was now expected to partake in some warped guessing game of "name that voice," and in a foreign language too.

"Come on Sarah. You can trust me," the voice wheedled as she heard the sound of the door rattling against the chain.

Oh yeah, well he'd be the first man who lived up to that label. She needed help, not long term promises he'd break tomorrow or the day after. She needed a strong arm to hang on to and perhaps some short term tenderness. She needed… Her grip on reality started to fade as her headache hit fever point and her ankle gave way from under her.

"Sarah, for God's sake remove the chain so I can help you," were the last words she heard that morning before sliding back on the floor in a heap.

Chapter Two

7th May. I still don't have a date for Saturday or a pair of shoes that I can actually wear. All I have is a thumping headache, a pair of black ballet pumps and an ankle the size of a turnip.

Her eyes snapped open to stare at the now familiar wood clad ceiling of her bedroom, so very different from her pristine white one in England with its Laura Ashley curtains and matching bedspread. Here she made do with a cheap white cover from the local supermarket but at least it was warm and snug as she raised her hand to the bruise on the back of her head.

She had no idea how or why she was still in bed, her fingers massaging the tender skin. She'd been having breakfast in her kitchenette and only gone outside to scatter some crumbs for the sparrows that visited each morning…

Sitting up was easier than she thought, her eyes on the glass of water and the couple of tablets that lay beside it. There was a note too. Tablets downed she unfolded the paper, a piece torn from the pad she kept in the kitchen if she wasn't very much mistaken.

Rest ma petite chou. I'll check on you later.

Oh, sorry about your door.
Pascal x

She frowned at the note. Pascal? She didn't know anyone called Pascal, did she? The name had a familiar ring to it but she couldn't quite place it. Her frown deepened as she looked at the rest of the note, translating it as "my little cabbage."

With that, she flung back the covers only to find herself still in her dressing gown, the belt of which was now knotted in the most peculiar knot imaginable. With a little shrug, her eyes landed on her ankle or, to be exact the neat bandage that strapped it in place. Getting to her feet she hobbled into the lounge to find he'd had to dismantle the security chain to gain access. Funnily enough she didn't care. He hadn't ravished her or anything, her hands fiddling with the knot to no avail. After another five minutes of fiddling she resorted to cutting the belt in two before shrugging it off and heading into the minute bathroom. She never bothered with pyjamas so if he hadn't secured the gown tight she might be the one having to pick him up off the floor at the sight of all her wobbly bits, she mused, removing the bandage before rolling it up for later.

Later found her curled up on the sofa in an old pair of black leggings with holes at the knees and a faded black t-shirt, her hair loose around her shoulders. She had an unintentional day off, a rare thing and, after emailing her lecturer at the Sorbonne, she sat with her leg up as she scrolled through her iPad for some way out of her dilemma. She needed a date for the weekend and frankly she was desperate. There was no one in college she wanted to ask, for no other reason than she didn't want to lead them on. And she wasn't into relationships, she never had been.

As an only child brought up by a string of nannies before being offloaded to boarding school, she'd learnt not to trust anyone but herself. There'd been that brief fling her first year in university with Paul, which had ended in disaster and, at the grand old age of nineteen, she'd decided she wasn't girlfriend material. If she couldn't trust herself to pick a decent partner from the millions out there, then she was better off by herself. But that didn't help her now.

Half an hour later found her throwing her iPad across the coffee table in disgust. She'd found several balding men coming to Paris for the weekend on business that she could hitch up with if extramarital sex was her thing. She'd even found a few prepared to marry her on the strength of her passport. But men she could present to her parents as a possible partner -

no chance. Was it true all the eligible men were already taken? What a depressing thought.

She only stirred at the sound of a thump on the door.

He looked even bigger now she was in bare feet, bigger and more approachable standing as he was with his hands full of the largest bouquet of cream roses she'd ever seen. Her eyes widened, her lips pulling into a gentle smile as she wondered if he was married, in need of a passport or both.

"How are you feeling? How's the ankle?"

She pulled out of her reverie with a jerk and, placing the flowers by the sink, waved a hand to the only chair as her manners kicked in. She wasn't in the mood for company, male or female but she couldn't very well throw him out after he'd rescued her and brought flowers too.

"Oh much better. Thank you for..." A frown appeared as she settled herself on the sofa. "How did you..?"

"Oh my men keep an eye on what's happening. They spotted you hadn't moved for a while and..."

"And you came to my rescue. Well, thank you again." Her eyes shifting to the flowers, "and for the roses, they're beautiful."

"You're welcome."

Her forehead wrinkled as she watched him move to sit beside her, lifting her leg on to his lap as if it was made of china. She didn't know what he was playing at but the weight of his hand on her leg as he examined her ankle was certainly playing havoc with her insides.

"It's better, yes?" His eyes meeting hers.

"Much, thank you. I must have twisted it when..."

"When?" He interrupted.

"I like to feed the birds." She raised her chin a little in case he thought her childish, but he only smiled.

"So do I."

"Sarah."

"Pascal." Their voices ringing out in unison.

"You first."

She'd only been going to offer him a drink anyway. Instead she scooped up her hair, allowing it to tumble over her shoulder. She always played with her hair when she was nervous and she'd never felt as nervous as she did now. She could count on one hand the number of times she'd been alone with a man and Pascal wasn't any man; he was her dream man.

Nestling back into the sofa she allowed her thoughts to admit what they'd been screaming out for the last three weeks. She fancied him rotten and, as he was here he must at least like her a little, maybe more than a little as she remembered the roses. Builders didn't get paid well, even senior ones. What had he called them again?

My men.

If he was the boss, he'd still be on a pittance compared to someone like Rupert, for example. Her lip curled at the unwelcome intrusion of Rupert who was something high in banking. She'd much prefer a man high up on scaffolding with muscles rippling in the heat, even if he probably couldn't afford a suit let alone a single rose. There were an awful lot of roses, her eyes flickering over to where she'd propped them up against the washing-up bowl.

He lowered her leg to rest back down, his hand still resting on her calf. But she had the funny feeling he wasn't aware of what he was doing, something she was sure of when his gaze finally landed on hers.

"I'd like to take you out to dinner when your leg's better, perhaps at the weekend?"

Her hand automatically reached up to twist the end of her hair as she considered her reply. This felt right somehow. His long tapering fingers circling the sole of her foot, his skin surprisingly smooth for someone used to working with their hands. But would it be right, him crammed in a shirt and tie trying to make small talk across the table? There was a wealth of difference having this sexy man rescue her like some damsel in a Richard Gere movie and having him make small talk with her parents. They'd want to know what he did and be awfully polite when they realised he was one of those grubby commoners they'd heard talk of.

Here she was desperate for a date at the weekend, more than desperate and here one turns up on her doorstep, even if he had decided to take the door apart first. She should jump at the chance being as he was the only one offering. He was good looking and suave in that sexy way only French men could be. He didn't look married either, which was always a plus, her gaze hovering over his left hand. He probably had a girl in every port, or should that be on every rooftop? But as it was only for dinner that shouldn't be a problem, should it?

She bit on her lower lip, well aware he was still staring at her while he waited for her answer. She could always make something up for her parents benefit, something to do with cultural differences if he did something mega embarrassing like slurp his soup, but first she needed to ask him something.

"Why?"

"Why not?"

"But I don't even know you?" Her head tilted away, her eyes now focussed on the building across the street, his building.

"So what do you want to know, Sarah? My age? My bank balance? My shoe size?" His voice hiding anger within its folds. "All I need to know is that I've wanted to kiss you for weeks, ever since I first saw you hauling all those cases out of the taxi."

His intense honeycomb coloured eyes imprisoned her to the sofa with a power she was helpless to resist, with a power she didn't want to resist. She wanted nothing more right now than the pressure of his lips against hers and yet all those things, all those other things, whilst not important to her were important to her parents; apart from the shoe size that is.

She shouldn't have opened the door to him and she certainly shouldn't have invited him in although, with the chain still in a pile on the table, she'd had little choice.

He lifted a hand and, cradling her chin, moved his head a little closer. She knew he was about to kiss her and there was nothing she could do to stop him except perhaps ask him not to.

With her pulse exploding in her ears, she felt her desire to do anything other than lift her lips to his overtake any last vestige of common sense. She wanted those lips to plunder hers and yet she couldn't allow that to happen.

Dragging her gaze away was difficult but not impossible as the image of Paul and what he'd done to her imprinted itself on her brain, and this was no Paul. This was some crummy builder with too much sex appeal for his own good. Her anger flared to match his as she remembered how damaging Paul's little stunt had been. There was no way she would allow herself get into that position again.

"And what if I said I wanted you to leave?"

His eyes flickered from her parted lips to her t-shirt and the way it strained against her breasts before returning to her face. "I'd say you're a liar."

He released her chin, his gaze never leaving hers. "I'm sorry, I shouldn't have said that." He ran his hand through his hair with a rueful grin. "You must have your reasons..."

She couldn't believe how bereft she was at the loss. She'd been psyching herself up for the kiss of all kisses only for him to turn all honourable on her. This man was a complete enigma, but if it was a competition, he'd just passed the first test with glowing colours. The only problem was she was pretty sure what the prize was going to be.

Struggling to her feet was difficult but she managed, one hand clinging on to the side of the sofa, all the time aware of his amber gaze following her every movement.

"Well I should go…"

"Pascal," she said, her voice causing him to pause, her words making him turn back. "I'm making myself a coffee, would you like one?"

"If you're sure?" He raised his eyebrow, one hand now holding the chain. "I can fix this while the kettle's boiling."

"And I'd like to go out for dinner with you, if you'd still like to?"

"It would be my pleasure." He knelt on the floor pulling a small screw driver from his back pocket only to pause.

"And Sarah?"

She paused on the way to the kitchen.

"29, 500 Euro's and 45."

"What?"

"My age, bank balance and shoe size."

"So about my parents," she said, adjusting the skirt of her dress over her knees before pleating the rich silver silk between restless fingers.

"Ah yes, your parents." She watched as he lowered the handbrake. "When I invited you out for dinner, I didn't quite realise I'd be inviting your parents along too. It's an old English custom I take it?"

Playing for time, her eyes lingered on where his hand rested on the gear stick. She was still getting over the shock of seeing him turn up in a suit, not to mention a red E Type Jaguar. He'd been hot in cut-off denims but now he was positively smoking in grey pinstripe and a snowy white shirt with coordinating black and white striped tie.

She'd hazard a guess at Saville Row for the suit and Jermyn Street for the shirt only because they had that little touch of something that set them apart. The way the jacket embraced his shoulders without a wrinkle, emphasising their breadth. But there was no way she could ask him where he got his clothes from. Hired? Borrowed? Stolen? It was best not to ask. When she'd admired the car, he'd smiled and told her his Lotus was in for a service. Mmm.

"Not quite. While my parents are old-fashioned, they're not that old-fashioned."

"Why then?" his tone dry, presumably with a head full of the thousand reasons for her parents chaperoning her on this their first date with not a hope of any of them being near the truth. It was good of him to go along with her idea for dinner. He'd probably planned a quiet tête-à-tête in one of the little street café's along the river and not the magical mystery tour she'd taken him on. Despite being dressed to impress, she was still unsure what his reaction would be when the 'little hotel her parents were staying in' turned out to be the Ritz.

With a sigh, she decided to tell him the truth. They were ships that passed in the night and there was nothing he'd be able to do with the information now her parents would be there.

"It's my birthday soon."

"When, *ma chérie?*"

She smiled at the endearment. Being on the edge of "The Luvvies Set" herself, she knew it meant nothing, but it felt good to be cherished all the same, even if it was only transitory, so much nicer than being called darling, or a cabbage come to that.

"Oh, that's not really relevant. The only relevant part is, if I'm not engaged by my birthday I'll miss out on inheriting quite a tidy sum from my late aunt."

He remained silent. Negotiating the traffic around the *Arc de Triomphe* even at this time of the evening was always difficult. But she was glad of the silence, her hand reaching up to fiddle with a loose curl over her ear.

"She was quite a character, Aunt Popsy; an irascible old dear but with a heart of gold. She left me everything but only on the proviso that I'm engaged to the man of my dreams by my twenty-third birthday and if not, it will all go to the Battersea Dog's Home."

"This er Battersea..?"

"Battersea Dog's Home. It's a world famous animal rescue shelter."

"*D'accord*, and you haven't met the man you want to marry, is that where I come in?"

Her hand fluttered on his arm before resuming its place on her lap. "I'm not getting married Pascal and I don't really care what happens to the money but…" She paused, her head now turned to look at the light sparkling out from what looked like a thousand candelabras brandishing the side of the hotel.

"But you don't want to upset your parents?" His hand reached out and rested on her knee. "I've had parents, I know how it works."

No you don't. You have no idea how it works.

But she let it go. He'd find out soon enough, and she'd be lucky if he stayed for the sweet.

She had to give him his due, he hardly missed a step at the sight of both her father and Rupert standing up from the table. The only sign he gave at the unwelcome extra man was a slight squeeze on her elbow as he propelled her towards them. Her mother didn't stand but then she never would, entrenched as she was in the social etiquette of a bygone era.

"Hello darling, vintage Dior, how clever of you," her eyes scanning the knee length sheath of a dress with interest.

"Hello Mother. Not really. The roads in Paris are heaving with the most adorable second-hand clothes shops," she said, reaching up to kiss her father's cheek before nodding to Rupert.

"Pre-loved darling, not second-hand; second-hand is so…"

"Common?" She glanced across the table. "You didn't say that Rupert would be joining us, Mother?" She added, struggling to keep her voice calm, but ice creeping in all the same.

"He had to pop over on business and as the plane takes four..," her eyes shifting to Pascal. "Introduce your friend, darling," a slight censure in her tone.

"Oh, of course." Turning, the smile froze on her lips as she realised she had no idea of his name, or indeed anything about him and he bloody well knew it, his eyes twinkling back. There was only one way to play it and that was fib. After all, she wasn't going out with him again. Her heart dropped at the thought.

"Pascal, I'd like to present my parents, The Earl and Countess Cosgrave, and Rupert

Reynolds-Smythe. Mum, dad, Rupert, this is Pascal…"

"de Sauvarin, Pascal de Sauvarin." He interrupted smoothly, "It's an honour to meet you both." His English as faultless as his smile.

"Sauvarin?" Her father interrupted, his eyes questioning. "Any relation to the Marquis de Sauvarin?"

"Only distant, I'm afraid."

"Old money that, very old," he added, narrowing his gaze in Rupert's direction. "I met him, let me see..," his hands steepled together on the white linen. "It must have been twenty years ago. The family residence was a pile outside Versailles with more turrets than sense."

"A very distant connection." He replied, placing his hand protectively along the back of Sarah's chair.

Rupert turned a sharp eye across the table. "It's very good of you to have escorted Lady Sarah for the evening; I hate to think of her in Paris all alone."

"She's not alone," he drawled, his hand curling around her neck in the most intimate of caresses. "Lady Sarah has me."

"Really?" His gaze flickering between them before settling on her. "You never mentioned it?"

He'd found her hand and, raising it up above the table pressed a kiss on to the soft skin before resting their entwined fingers on the table. "Does she have to mention it, er, Rupert?"

Sarah's head flew from side to side at the jibe even as she felt the warmth of his hand generate little shivers of anticipation up her arm.

Oh God, they'll come to fisticuffs soon.

Her father wouldn't intervene now he had the wine menu to peruse whilst her mother was no use. She'd spent the last ten minutes trying to work out if the woman at the next table was wearing real pearls. She could have told her without having to turn her head. No one wore fake jewels at the Ritz.

Sighing with relief at the sight of the head waiter arriving with their menus, she reclaimed her hand before starting a rambling conversation about the benefits of lobster over steak when she didn't care a fig for either. In truth, she'd lost her appetite when Rupert and his flabby flushed face stood up to greet her. She knew what her mother was up to but couldn't she come up with something better than a fifty-three-year old divorcé with a drink problem?

She hadn't been lying when she'd said she didn't care about the money. The thought of all those millions freaked her out. She'd won a scholarship for her year at the Sorbonne and that, added to the allowance her parents gave her for keeping out of their hair allowed her to be independent, something she wouldn't give up with a struggle. Marriage to Rupert would mean exchanging her freedom for a prison; a gilded one with all the trappings of wealth, but a prison all the same.

"*Chérie*?" The weight of his arm interrupted her thoughts and, glancing away from Rupert, she threw him a little smile.

"I'm fine; it's just I have a headache coming on." She pulled a brief smile at her mother's questioning stare. "Perhaps the lady in the restroom will have some paracetamol?"

"I'll come with you, darling." Her mother rose to her feet, closely followed by all the men, including Pascal. "We'll leave you to your business talk." She tittered, linking arms with her daughter.

They'd scarcely left the table when her mother started on her.

"Well, if I'd known you were going to arrive with THAT on your arm, I'd have left poor old Rupert at home. Clever you."

"Shush Mother, they'll hear you!" Sarah replied, twisting her head briefly to find both her father and Rupert leaning across the table with serious intent.

"No they won't. They'll be busy interrogating that handsome hunk of yours. You know your father won't give his permission for you to marry just anyone!"

"I didn't think I'd need it."

"Now darling, you know we're only trying to protect your best interests don't you? After that Paul person, we can't be too careful," she added, tipping her handbag out in search of lip gloss.

Paul had been the one fly in her ointment on the road to independence. She should have guessed the way he'd latched on to her that there had to be an ulterior motive. There was nothing about her to attract the instant attention of the best looking man on campus apart from the news of an heiress on site. He'd wined and dined her, and would have managed to do a lot more if she hadn't overheard him bragging about his soon to be paid off student loan.

"Paul was a very long time ago, Mother. I can scarcely remember what he looked like," she replied and realised the truth in her words. She'd thought herself in love, so much in love that she'd nearly considered ignoring the fact he was only after her money, and now he was nothing; just some petty little teenage crush.

"Your father knew all about him," her mother murmured, adding a thin rim of eyeliner to her lower lids.

"What?"

"Mmm and give him a day or two and he'll know all about this Pascal de Sauvarin of yours."

"Now hold on a minute…"

"Darling, when you're a mother you'll understand." She patted her shoulder with a smile. "Good looks and a fantastic body aren't everything." She gave herself one final look in the mirror before adding. "Although I must admit I didn't think you had it in you."

"Had what in me?" Sarah was hastily swallowing the couple of paracetamol the attendant had found.

"Finding such a perfect specimen, and what lovely manners for such a young man, obviously public school, and that tie…"

"His tie, what's wrong with his tie?"

"It's so 'Oxbridge' darling. I think Magdalen but ask your father, he knows about these things."

"Oh really." Her voice weak, even as she wondered if that's why his English was so good – too good. "We haven't discussed universities…"

"No of course you haven't," she said, the titter back. "What's he like in bed?"

"Mother!"

Looking at her father in deep conversation with Pascal, she felt a sudden urge to be back in her pocket-handkerchief of an apartment with distant views over the Seine. Her headache was now pounding with a relentless determination and, if she didn't leave straight away, she'd scream. There were so many questions, too many questions; unanswerable questions she knew her father and now Pascal would be adept at evading.

Who was this Pascal she'd consented to spend the evening with? His manners came straight out of Downton Abbey and she was certain now his suit wasn't some *off the peg* piece of tat. Either he was a consummate actor, or born with a whopping silver spoon in his mouth and for the life of her she couldn't work out which.

Stumbling to her feet, she almost laughed at the sight of all three men following her like string puppets. She'd come with Pascal and she'd leave with him, that was the rule but she didn't have to speak to him more than that.

"I'm sorry for breaking up the party but my headache…" Her eyes throwing out a silent appeal to her mother who, for once in her life, didn't let her down.

"Oh poor Sarah," tipping her head towards Pascal. "She used to get the most frightful headaches as a child. You need to tuck her up in bed with the blinds down and she'll be as right as rain in the morning." Turning back, she added, "I'll phone you first thing tomorrow, darling."

She tried to leave him outside but he was having none of it. He took the key from her fingers and, opening the door, gently pushed her through before heading for the bedroom and turning down the duvet all the time muttering to himself.

"This is becoming a habit."

"What?"

I said this is becoming a habit, me helping you into bed." He was lifting her dressing gown off the hook behind the door so missed the look on her face. "I take it you sleep in the nude?"

"Excuse me!"

"Well you weren't wearing…"

"That's my business." She snatched the dressing gown from his hands, her face the colour of an overripe tomato.

"I'm not sure where the belt is though?" he said, scanning the floor.

"I couldn't get the knot undone…"

"Ah yes, now I remember." He smiled, his face a picture of innocence. "I er seem to remember having some difficulty in getting it to stay closed." He made his way towards her. "I'll be off then, unless you want me to tuck you in?"

"There's little chance of that. This really is a thumper," her hand to her brow.

"Poor Sarah." He frowned down at her. "Would you like me to stay?' He added, lifting his head to look at the sofa. "Perhaps you shouldn't be alone? That was a nasty crack you gave yourself…"

"I'm fine, Pascal. I'm used to looking after myself." She managed a small smile. "Thank you for…"

"Thank you for pretending to be my boyfriend, was that what you were going to say, Lady Sarah? Thank you for not reaching across the table and punching Rupert's lights out for the way he assumed you were his property? It was my pleasure, but next time no surprises, huh?"

"Hold on a minute…"

"No, you hold on a minute, Sarah." His voice harsh, but the hands that reached out and cradled her face were soft, so soft as he smoothed the pads of his thumbs across her cheeks. "I played your little game and without you telling me any of the rules beforehand, now it's my turn."

"Your turn?" She repeated.

"Don't be scared little one," his hands now moving to caress the back of her neck. "Whilst I'd love to join you for what's left of the night I'll wait until I'm asked." His hands paused, his eyes wavering between her mouth and her eyes as if he was trying to make his mind up about something before finally pushing her backwards through the door. "I'll pick you up at seven."

Chapter Three

*11th May. A day's shopping to look forward
to and today I'm looking for something sexy.
The grey had been fine but with the neck up to
my chin and sleeves down to my wrist I looked
like a throwback from the last century, or
should that be the century before?*

Sarah loved Saturday mornings in Paris most
of all. She loved the joy of being able to wake
up late, just as she loved the joy of being able
to languish for as long as she liked under the
warmth of her duvet; only sneaking out of bed
when her body screamed for coffee and
croissants.

Sliding her feet to the floor she slipped her
arms into her robe before tying a loose knot
with the scarf she'd improvised instead of the
belt she'd thrust to the bottom of the bin.
Padding into the kitchen she flicked on the
kettle before wandering over to her tiny
balcony.

With her elbows on the wrought-iron
railings, she ignored the now quiet building
opposite. Instead, she craned her neck for that
distant view of the river and the gentle flow of
tugs and pleasure cruisers before turning her

attention to the building site. She was annoyed at the way her gaze automatically pulled in that direction, for in truth there was little to see except bare scaffolding rods and a pile of grey bricks. But she continued to stare, her imagination filling in enough gaps to keep her attention pinned all day if necessary.

It was only the click of the kettle that drew her attention back to the task in hand, but within minutes she found herself back outside, all her thoughts on one thing.

She didn't get him and that annoyed her. She didn't get him and she didn't understand why that worried her. She was off men for good, wasn't that the promise she'd made herself after Paul? If it hadn't been for sneaking up behind him in the canteen with every intention of surprising him, she wouldn't have heard him bragging about how he'd snared an heiress. She'd never let on she'd heard, instead she deleted him from her phone, her Facebook account, her life as if he'd never existed. He'd been hurt at first; hurt closely followed by aggressive. But when he finally realised he'd lost he'd done the worst thing possible.

Finding out the man you loved was only after one thing was bad enough but to have her supposed sex life splattered all over the tabloids was difficult to stomach. She was used to all the media attention just as she was used to keeping a close tab on her private life. But since then, apart from Cara, she'd kept her own council and stayed out of the limelight unless it was dinner with her parents.

Raising her mug to her lips, her eyes scrolled over the empty platform, her imagination playing tricks on her in the bright sunlight. She could almost see him dipping down to pick up another block, his muscles bracing against the weight. She couldn't quite decide which version of him she preferred: Pascal the sexy builder with bulging biceps or *Monsieur de Sauvarin*, the composite gentleman with unquestionable taste in both clothes and ties. She'd have to make a point of spending as much time in his company as possible to find out. It would be a hardship, a huge self-sacrifice even but she was game if he was.

It was obvious he fancied her, she mused, securing the scarf tighter around her waist. He fancied her just like she fancied him. But he was honourable enough not to do anything about it at present. She blushed at the thought of him carrying her into bed, her fingers skimming over the very thin silk of her cream dressing gown bought because she liked it and not for any warmth giving properties. If she'd wanted warmth she'd have bought velour but, for all her mother's faults, she'd taught her well. There were some things more important than warmth as she smoothed the silky fabric across her thighs and velour, for all its commendable properties, just didn't do it for her.

Resting her empty mug back on the table she made her way into the lounge. She'd been press-ganged into accepting his invite for this evening but then again she owed him for keeping her away from Rupert. However that didn't mean she couldn't arm herself with some information about this elusive man with more sex appeal than was good for her. She couldn't very well find out about his suit unless she could think of a way of checking out the label. But she knew his name and hadn't her mother thought she'd recognised his tie?

Half an hour later and she was outside waiting for her mother to collect her. It hadn't taken her more than five minutes to find out that the tie was indeed from Magdalen College, but as knowledge went, it didn't help her. College ties were two a penny if you knew which sites to buy them from. She'd also searched his name with as much success. While Pascal de Sauvarin wasn't as common as Jean Martin (the French equivalent of John Smith) it was too common for her to pin him down. She'd found three in Paris alone, but none of them sounded right.

There was a hotshot lawyer married with three kids with offices in the Pigalle. An accountant with a balding pate and moustache and finally an up and coming architect making a name for himself with his bold designs and flair for the unusual. But there were no builders or developers, her mind swinging back to that comment about *"My men."* She'd finally given up. She could spend the rest of the day worrying what type of man she'd agreed to spend the evening with, or she could concentrate on trying to find something decent to wear.

The truth of it was, apart from the silver dress, she had nothing suitable in her wardrobe for any kind of impromptu date. There were jeans and leggings galore and an assortment of the long floaty tops she favoured with an array of chunky cardigans but that was it, so today she'd agreed to meet her mother for a little last minute shopping followed by lunch at some in-vogue posh restaurant.

They spent the morning going from one dress shop to another where her mother seemed to be on a mission to spend as much money as possible.

"What about this, darling?" She asked, holding up a bright red mini skirt and matching crop top.

"Really! I wouldn't be seen dead in it."

"Not for you Sarah, for me," she added, holding the skirt up to her slim frame.

"Are you trying to give Father a heart attack?" She queried.

"Mmm you're probably right." She returned it to the rail, "although if I was ten years younger…" Plucking a long black skirt off its hanger she passed it across with a smile. "Now this is your size, and your colour." She added with a shake of her head. "Why all you girls wear black is beyond me."

"Because it goes with everything." Sarah held up the skirt, liking its full long layers on sight. "How much is…?"

"Oh, don't worry about that, your father will be more than happy to treat you." She waved a hand towards the lingerie department. "Choose something lacy to go with it. I'm sure Pascal will be appreciative."

"Mother!"

"So tell me how you met?"

They were sitting in a little restaurant on the Rue de Rivoli with glasses of crisp chardonnay in front of them.

"Oh, he works opposite, so we sort of bumped into each other."

"You didn't tell me what he does? Some kind of banking like Rupert?"

"No, nothing like that. He's in construction."

"Oh, like an engineer."

"Yes, something like that." She took a large sip of wine while the waiter presented her mother with a plain green salad before setting a large bowl of mussels and French fries in front of her.

She smiled across the table as her mother picked up a lettuce leaf with a frown. "Go on, help yourself."

"I don't know where you get your metabolism from," she grumbled, stealing a chip and the smallest mussel. "It's not fair."

"And remember I'm out for dinner too." She dipped a chunk of bread into the bowl, her smile breaking into a grin.

Her mother groaned. "So is this thing with Pascal serious? Should I start planning your wedding?"

"It's a little early for that, mother."

"Poor Rupert, he'll be devastated. He's loved you for so long."

"Mother, how can you say that! He's only after my money."

"That's a little harsh, Sarah. He's got quite enough of his own."

"I thought you said his wife took him to the cleaners?"

"Well she did get a few million off him, but men like that bounce back. Your father and I thought he'd be ideal…"

"Mother, I don't love him. I don't even like him."

"I can see why now, darling." She sat back and smiled at the couple of chips Sarah had balanced on the edge of her plate. "If I were you, I'd have chosen Pascal too; all that raw energy and brains to match." She picked up the chip and chewed the end her eyes on Sarah's face. "Your father liked him, said he had a sound business mind which, coming from your father as you know, means a lot."

"Well don't get your hopes up too far. I still have no intention of getting married anytime soon."

"But, darling?"

"But nothing, Mother. I've never been worried about the money."

"Sarah, how can you say that?"

"Very easily. As long as I have enough to live on…" She stood up and pressed a hand on mother's shoulder before pressing a kiss against her perfumed cheek. "Thank you for lunch and for the clothes, but if I don't go now I'll be late."

"Wow, this is fabulous." Her eyes roamed around the cave-like interior of The Club de Jazz.

"Yes, it is," his voice low in his throat as he watched her slip her arms out of her jacket. He'd thought her beautiful yesterday in her cutesy little sheath dress with high collar and long sleeves, but this evening she looked amazing.

He'd said not to dress up, and she hadn't but the tight black ribbed t-shirt embraced her flesh like a second skin, a skin he was having difficulty in not stretching out to touch. She'd teamed it with a long, black, handkerchief-hemmed skirt and low-heeled patent shoes with the most adorable ankle straps imaginable, even as his mind wondered if she was a stockings or tights kind of girl.

Clenching his jaw so his back teeth ground together he took her jacket before pulling out her chair, his mind trying and failing to move away from the loop it had got itself into; a loop where his hand reached under the table and went on an intrepid exploration all of its own. Only by clenching his fists, in addition to his teeth, did he gain any semblance of control over both his mind and his body.

Her gaze wandered back to his, and he wondered for the umpteenth time what it was about her that got him right in the solar plexus? She took his breath away each time he saw her and, if it carried on, he'd have to think of some method of alternative supply like an oxygen cylinder, his lips pulling into a rueful smile.

It wasn't that she was beautiful in the accepted sense. Her sapphire blue eyes were wide and expressive but her lips a little too wide for any accepted images of beauty, but oh so plump and kissable as he watched her little white teeth grab onto her lower lip. She was a little too short, barely up to his shoulders but her figure was all and more with well-rounded breasts and hips made for stroking. His mind went back to that morning in the apartment where he'd found her unconscious on the floor. Even with the retied belt he couldn't help but notice the thin silk accentuating rather than hiding every plane and curve.

"Pascal?" Her voice queried softly, a frown appearing.

"Sorry, *ma chérie*, I was miles away." He grinned, hoping against hope she wasn't a mind reader or she'd be slapping his face and storming off. "What would you like to drink? Wine, lager?"

"Oh, wine, please as we're both not driving. Any colour."

"Mon Dieu, sacrilège!"

"Excuse me?" Her eyes wide.

"Non. Inexcusable. To a Frenchman the colour of wine is most important. We'll start with a couple of glasses of kir royale." His hands placing the wine menu back in the little plastic folder as he threw her a look from under raised eyebrows. "I take it you like champagne?"

"Who doesn't?"

"*Très bon*, and after I'll feed you."

"I can't wait." Her voice dry.

"You're teasing me," he replied with a smile before turning to the waiter with his order.

"Me, tease a Frenchman? More than my life's worth, Pascal." Her eyes twinkling across at him.

Resting his chin in his hands he continued to study her, his eyes roaming across her face as if he was trying to imprint it to memory. "So tell me about you, about Lady Sarah Cosgrave."

"There's nothing to tell. You know most of it already." She shifted back in her seat.

"Not the important things. So why the Sorbonne? Why Paris? Surely it's a long way from home and family?"

"Perhaps it's because it is such a long way…" She caught his eye but only briefly. "I like my own company and when I won the scholarship..."

"Oh, talented as well."

"Talented as well as what?" Her eyes narrowed, but he let her fill in her own gaps, which she did on a blush. He liked it when she blushed.

"Let's play a game, Sarah." He paused, his gaze searching hers with a frown. "I take it I can call you Sarah or do I have to use the L…"

"Just Sarah is fine."

"Well, Just Sarah, as I was saying, what about a getting to know you game?" He watched the wary expression back in her eyes and he wondered who'd hurt her, his gut clenching at the thought. She'd been hurt and he was pretty sure it was a man that had done the hurting. She'd tell him in her own time, he just hoped it was sooner rather than later.

"Okay," she replied, taking refuge in the tall champagne flute in front of her.

"I get to ask a question and then you get to ask one. No tricks. I'll even be a gentleman and let you go first. Be gentle with me."

Their eyes locked. "Which university did you attend?"

"Ah, intelligent, beautiful and talented. I must keep my wits about me." He smiled, resting back in his chair as he started to enjoy himself. "It's universities actually." He added and watched her eyes grow wide. "Like you, I won a scholarship - to Magdalen, but before that I studied at Rennes, which is-"

"In Brittany." She offered him a smile. "We used to spend our holidays in La Baule. What did you…?"

"*Non non*," he waved a finger at her. "It's my turn, *ma chérie*. What instrument do you carry around in that enormous case of yours?"

"The saxophone."

"Mmm that figures." He stroked his chin, his eyes widening. "It's heavy enough."

"And what did you read?" She repeated, her voice filled with laughter.

"Ah yes. I'm an architect." He noticed the way her head gave a little nod of affirmation. So she'd been searching him up. Good. Two could play at that game. He'd spent half the night reading up on her, although there was little to be found apart from some nonsense from a few years ago and that photo of her sitting alone in a Parisian café. He wanted to know more. He wanted to know everything.

"So what about your family, Sarah? I've met your parents but are there more?"

"That's more than one question." Her mouth twitching as she played with the stem of her glass. "No, there's only me and my parents.

There are horses of course, which are sort of family too but I had quite a solitary upbringing and my parents… Well, you can tell the type of people they are: loving but distant is how I'd best describe them. There's a godfather, Uncle George, but I don't see him much. He went into the church." She took a long sip from her drink, leaving a faint shimmer of lipstick against the rim before lifting her eyes to his.

"If wasn't for Hopper and Mrs Hopper I'd have turned into a right tearaway."

"Hopper and," he raised an eyebrow before continuing. "What is this hopper?"

"Not what, whom." She lifted the corners of her mouth into a smile. "Hopper is our butler, and he's married to Beverley, the best cook in the world," she expanded. "I know it probably sounds all very upper-class to the uninitiated but without Hopper and his wife, I'd still be roaming the estate climbing trees and scrumping for apples." She smiled, catching his eye. "I was a tom boy."

"I can imagine!"

"And your family, Pascal? I was half expecting you to bring them along for an introduction?"

"Ah, it won't be a long answer I'm afraid. I don't have any."

"That's very remiss of you. So you're a foundling?"

"A founding?" His voice holding a question.

"A foundling, it's another term for an orphan. You know, someone with no parents." Her eyes meeting his with a beguiling softness to melt the most determined of hearts. But his didn't need melting. It lay in a puddle at the bottom of his chest just waiting for a look, a smile to jump start it back to life.

"*Non* Sarah, you misunderstand. They're both dead now. Even my uncles and aunts; all dead, so I have no family."

"What, no cousins, nephews?"

"*Non.*"

"Well that's unusual, as well as very sad." She patted his hand. "If you ever feel in the need of some, I'll happily lend you mine."

"*Merci,* but I'm not in need of family. Or at least I wasn't," his voice trailing away to nothing as he plucked the menu from its stand. "So what do you fancy?"

You, that's what I fancy,
You with all those delicious French trimmings thrown in for free like your sexy accent and come to bed eyes; like your taut muscles that no plain white shirt and tan chinos could ever have a hope in hell of camouflaging.

Yep, she'd decided to have him for both main course and dessert as soon as she'd spotted him on her landing, and she wouldn't even be in need of a spoon! As soon as she'd opened the door all her inhibitions and hang-ups flew out the window, along with her pride, and any worries of him being an heiress hunter. Life, that yesterday had been boring with a capital B, was now full of the most amazing possibilities, all of which included him.

She picked up the menu he was holding, his fingers brushing against hers with a sensual familiarity that had her heart hammering under her ribs. Dampening her response with a sigh she scanned the list of foods like a good girl when all she wanted to do was grab his hands, both of them, pull him out of the club and back to her apartment. Instead she ended up agreeing to a shared platter of spicy Buffalo wings and a side order of French fries.

Ordering out of the way she nestled back against her chair and toyed with a second glass of kir royale that had miraculously appeared in front of her. The music started up and assaulted what was left of her senses with a rendition of one of her favourite pieces by Debussy "The girl with the flaxen hair."

The club had gone from buzzing one second to absolute silence the next as all eyes pinned themselves to the solitary man on the little stage in the corner with only his saxophone for company. The audience silence was broken by loud clapping and cheering as he slipped into "Careless Whisper." She finally dragged her gaze away at the sight of their food only to find him staring at her again. She almost lifted her hand to check on her hair, which she'd left trailing over one shoulder in a loose plait but she resisted the temptation. Instead, she picked out a wing before pushing the plate in his direction.

"So, can you play as good as that?" he asked, choosing a couple of chips and dipping them in the accompanying mayonnaise. "Because if you can, I'm telling you now I'm giving up work and becoming your manager."

She laughed. "I wish. Not about the manager bit, about the being as good as..."

"I got that, Sarah. I don't think I'm brave enough to manage you, or indeed any woman."

"I wouldn't have put you down as a coward?"

"Not a coward, just sensible. I'd only come off worse." His soulful gaze met hers.

"You'll have me reaching for a violin in a minute." Her eyes creasing at the corners.

"French men are very emotional Sarah. It's best not to tease us, especially with a chin covered in barbeque sauce," he added, wiping her skin with his finger before raising it to her lips for her to lick, his eyes never leaving her face.

"Oh, thank you, I should have chosen something easier to eat." She picked up a serviette and scrubbed at her face, careful to avoid her mouth where the lingering pressure from his fingers left an invisible trail of sensations. "All gone now?"

He nodded. "Sometimes in life its best to go for what you want. There'll always be good men about to help you if you get a little messy." His eyes flickering back to her mouth.

"And are you a good man, Pascal?" she questioned, her hand trembling as she scrunched up the napkin before placing it on the side of her dish.

"That's not for me to say. I'll never do anything intentional to hurt you if that's what you mean," he said, fanning his hands out across the table. "But I'm far from being a saint."

"I'm not after a saint, but I'm not sure I'm after a relationship either." She pushed her plate away before draining the remains of her glass.

"Let's see where we end up, then" He stood up and beckoning to the waiter placed a few notes in the plastic dish that accompanied the bill. "Do you fancy a walk home along the Seine or a taxi? It's only a short stroll."

Of course it is. It's a short stroll along one of the most romantic parts of Paris; a stroll for lovers.

She knew what was going to happen in her mind's eye as clearly as if she was watching an action replay of her life on the big screen. But that didn't stop her from picking up her jacket and allowing him to help her into the sleeves before his arm rested across her shoulders.

As soon as they'd left the club she'd imagined him pausing under one of those ornate candelabra lampposts that punctuated the side of the river before pulling her into his arms, his mouth seeking hers. She could almost taste the kiss on her lips as his mouth increased its pressure even as her mind worked out the exact words she should use to ask him up for a coffee.

All around there were lovers doing exactly that, they'd even had to side step a couple doing quite a lot more than just kissing. But his hand had remained where it was, resting on the curve of her shoulder, his fingers heavy as they moulded to her skin. They'd reached her apartment in no time and now the words hovering on her lips deserted her as all the uncertainties and questions invaded her head as to why he'd backed off. She'd been sure he'd wanted her but now… now she felt the distance between them growing with every beat of her heart.

She tried to pull away, to increase the distance, but he was having none of it. Instead of letting go he jerked her within the circle of his arms for the tightest of embraces. His forehead rested gently on hers, his eyes hovering again over her lips: watching, waiting, wanting. After an interminable length he reached up both hands and, cradling her face with supple fingers, managed to find some words.

"What am I going to do about you *mignonne*?"

"I don't understand." But he'd placed a finger against her lips to silence her. "Spend the day with me tomorrow, Sarah - we'll go on a picnic?"

There was nothing she wanted more. Well, there was but it looked like he was going to be a gentleman, her gaze locking to his. She understood none of it, but she could live with that if only he'd kiss her.

He bent his head and her eyes fluttered closed, her lips parting in gentle expectation but she needn't have bothered. Instead of lips meeting lips, all she got was a firm kiss against each cheek before the final insult; one to the tip of her nose.

"Off to bed with you before I change my mind," he ended, opening the street door and pushing her through with the light touch of his hand.

Dragging her way up the stairs, a large part of her felt let down while the other part analysed just what he'd meant about changing his mind. The only thing she could come up with was that he was regretting offering to spend the day with her.

She'd psyched herself up for a very different end to her evening than a cup of cocoa and a cold bed but she couldn't argue that he wasn't gentlemanly, too gentlemanly. Where was the rough builder she'd imagined with hands like mitts crawling all over her? Where was the insatiable Frenchman who tumbled her into bed as soon as their lips met for the first time? Instead she'd ended up with a chivalrous architect, well she hadn't even ended up with him; she'd ended up all by herself.

Even Rupert, for all him being old enough to be her father had tried it on a few times until she'd told him in no uncertain terms she'd set the dogs on him if he tried it again. She'd only avoided being dragged into his arms that last time by insisting she wanted to wear white with impunity, which of course set off another whole set of problems.

Silent words floated around her head like 'hussy', 'tart' and even 'slapper' but she didn't care. Her fancying the pants off Pascal changed nothing. She still had no intention of getting married. But there was no reason why she couldn't enjoy life a little. There was nothing more boring, or sadder, than a middle-aged virgin.

Reaching the sanctuary of her apartment, she headed for the balcony to lean against the railings and stare out at the inky black night still buzzing with the distant sounds from the city. Her mind wandered back again to their walk where words had proved unnecessary. It was all a puzzle and, at this time of night, much too much of a puzzle for her to even begin to unravel.

Turning, she paused at the faint sound coming from the next balcony, a discordant note to the sultry Parisian tones echoing in the stillness. She frowned at the wall that separated one apartment from the other as the scratching noise repeated itself, this time louder. Eyes adjusted to the darkness all she could make out was a balcony; an empty balcony, which only a couple of days ago had been festooned with flower boxes and plants. Her neighbours, a sour faced couple, had presumably moved out because of the building work opposite. Come to think of it, she hadn't seen either of them around for a few days so if the apartment was empty, who or what was making all that noise?

She wouldn't be able to sleep until she found out.

Chapter Four

11th May. I never used to be clumsy, but my life's suddenly turned into a no go disaster zone - a no go disaster zone smelling of fish!

Merde!

She blinked in horror at the deep inky black bruise swelling on her shin. She knew she shouldn't have rushed off the balcony like a lunatic. She should have taken her time and avoided tripping over the leg of the chair but it was too late for that now, far too late as she watched in fascination as the bruise continued to stretch out through her skin like an inflating balloon. Perhaps if she closed her eyes it would go away. But when she reopened them the bruise had expanded to duck egg proportions.

God, what a disaster, she grumbled, limping towards the kitchen. She'd had her night all planned, that is after he'd dumped her on the doorstep, bed and the last chapter of her book. It wasn't the exciting end to the evening she'd hoped for but, as she'd been dumped… Was she being too hard on him? Did he dump her or just drop her off? And then she remembered the way he'd almost shoved her through the door like an unwanted parcel. No, she'd been dumped all right.

At least she now knew what it felt like, she thought, scrabbling around in the fridge-freezer for the bag of peas she knew she didn't have. But she wouldn't feel guilty about that. There were plenty of other things she could feel guilty about and… why didn't she have any peas? Peas didn't come high up on any of her list of priorities. Peas didn't feature at all, she thought, slamming the door closed.

She'd been hoping for some frozen vegetables to supplement the lack of peas, or at the very least ice cream, but it was exactly as she remembered; totally empty apart from that fish left over from last week's supper.

She'd invited Cara and Aaron around for *sole bonne femme* as a thank you for hiding her from the reporters and then helping her to move. However, the traditional French fayre she'd arranged hadn't gone as planned with Aaron describing in boring detail the difference between a vegetarian and a pescatarian. The final laugh was on him though as he'd ended up with a plate of green beans, being as distrustful of the cheese as he was of the fish. His loss was her gain she thought, lifting the solid fillet with a look of wry distaste stamped across her face. It was the fish or nothing!

Thankful at least for the rolled up bandage left over from her ankle she stripped off her stockings and, slapping the ice cold flesh against her shin, strapped it to her leg. Half hobbling to the bedroom, she threw on a pair of leggings well aware she still had to investigate that sound. It would have been easy if her neighbours were in, but five minutes of fruitless doorbell ringing had not provided any easy end to this fiasco of an evening.

She wasn't scared about what lay ahead, which was unusual being as heights weren't her thing. But any fear of traversing from balcony to balcony had deserted her when her shin had connected with the uncompromising metal of the chair. It was funny if anything. Instead of the night of passion she'd planned, she was about to the straddle the outside of her apartment with half a dead fish lashed to her leg.

Seconds later found her standing on the self-same chair as she placed her foot on the balcony railing. She was having second thoughts now but with one heave she found herself clinging to the side of the concrete wall with an outstretched arm and leg, the only things preventing her from falling to the pavement below. It was too late to change her mind so with eyes glued ahead she took a final leap and found herself on her bottom in the middle of next door's balcony.

She looked around the clearly deserted space with a sigh. Wherever the noise was coming from it was from inside. Peering through the glass into the bare lounge there was little to see in the blackness until she spotted dark eyes glinting yellow from the light of her torch.

Her stomach tightened at the thought of just what kind of ferocious beast lived inside. It could be anything, but with her luck it was probably some nasty banned breed with a bad case of sharp teeth disease.

She tried the latch only to find it ease under the weight of her hand. Being on the fourth floor and empty to boot they probably thought it was all right to leave it unlocked, she thought, hurrying in to discover the smallest skinniest runt of a cat she'd ever seen cowering in the corner. His eyes were huge, but that's the only thing that was.

Without a second to lose, she scooped him under her arm before heading out the front door, pleased she'd remembered at the last minute to leave her own door on the latch just in case someone had to rescue her for the second time in a week. Her mind resolutely didn't dwell on who her rescuer might be, or indeed under what circumstances he might need to barge into her apartment in the dark of night.

In truth, she was a coward at heart but a kind-hearted one. She'd known instinctively that the scratches were from some animal. She'd just hoped it was something larger than a rat and smaller than a horse. A cat she could manage, but a horse!

Arriving home, she placed the cat on the floor of the kitchen before offering him an impromptu supper of leftover croissants soaked in warm milk. Not the most nutritious of meals but the cat didn't seem to mind as, within seconds, the bowl was licked clean.

"That's enough for now, little one. It's too late to sort out a litter tray," she said, removing the bandage from her leg and placing the now defrosted fillet back in the fridge. Lifting him up with a gentle hand, she didn't have to tell him twice to snuggle up on the end of her bed before stripping off the rest of her clothes and joining him for what little was left of the night.

"It's only eight o'clock in the morning," she said, staring into the face of a wide awake not to mention wickedly handsome, Pascal even as she clutched her dressing gown tighter around her waist.

"So it is, but I have croissants," he wheedled, waving a fragrant bag in front of her nose.

"You'd better come in then." She walked ahead, picking up the clothes that still littered the floor from last night. "I have to warn you though I have a guest staying," she added over her shoulder with a smile.

"Really? What, one of your girlfriends…?"

"No actually, a boy." Enjoying his confusion, she watched his eyes shifting around the room before finally landing on the sofa.

"*Mon Dieu*. What do you call that?"

"It's a cat. *Une chat!*" she replied, her gaze following his to the grey bundle of fur. "What did you think it was?"

"The mangiest flea ridden cat it's ever been my displeasure to meet." His eyebrows rose. "So that's why the place smells of…?"

She blushed right up to the roots of her hair. Despite the shower and clean bed linen his screwed up nose was a good enough reminder as any that her little piece of French heaven stank like Billingates Fish Market.

Stalking over to the couch she ran a hand across the silky fur on his back. "He just needs a bit of care and attention, don't you boy," the sound of the microwave interrupting her. "I'll just go and…"

"He needs an awful lot more than care and attention," his eyes riveted to the way the cat"s back leg was scratching his stomach. "A dose of flea powder, not to mention worming tablets for a start."

"Don't be mean." She would have said more, but he interrupted her.

"Mmm nice."

She turned sharply to catch him picking up a stray stocking.

"Here, give me that," she snapped and, hand extended, pointed towards the kitchen. "I'm just going to get dressed…"

"Of course you are, take all the time in the world. I'll feed Tiddles shall I?"

"Tiddles?" She paused, throwing him a quick frown.

"Well, you're going to have to call him something, unless you've named him already?"

"Er no, we haven't gotten around to that. Name, food, litter tray…" A smile lifted the corners of her mouth. "Perhaps we should put off our picnic until I've had a chance to go shopping."

"No you don't! I'll sort out the necessary…" He interrupted. "What about *Minou*? He's far from a kitten but as he's starting a new life…"

"*Minou* it is."

She found him propped up against the balcony, the table set with an impromptu breakfast including both tea and coffee.

"I wasn't sure which you preferred." He quirked an eyebrow at her skinny jeans and purple and green flowing top, his gaze trailing down to her old sneakers. "I take it there are no stockings under there." He added with a frown.

"Behave yourself, and tea's fine thank you."

She sat down and he pulled out the chair opposite.

"You English, and your tea."

"I could say the same about you French and your coffee." Her glance flickered to the building opposite. "How much do you and your men drink anyway, you always seem to be having coffee breaks?"

"Ah, there's hope for me yet."

"What?"

"Well you've obviously noticed me, or is it one of my men?"

He was laughing at her, she just knew it and the most annoying thing was she'd walked straight into his trap. "I... I..." she stuttered.

"It's all right, *ma petite*. I feel the same way."

She had to change the subject, what with the way his eyes were hovering over her face again. She felt she was drowning. No, she felt like she was standing on the top of a precipice and his hand was just about to push her over. Glancing around she finally noticed Minou tucking into the remains of the fish, a bag of cat litter standing beside him.

"How did you manage to…?"

"Ah, us builders know everything."

"Really?" Her eyes wide. "But there's nowhere near enough to buy..."

"Buy? No, not buy; borrow. Madame Du Pont, the lady three doors along from you feeds her cats on her balcony every morning like clockwork. She was more than happy to supply a couple of tins and some spare cat litter," he added, pointing to the improvised plastic tray in the corner.

"Oh, and I haven't even met her."

"Well of course you haven't. The French are very private, but in an emergency the most helpful race around." He threw a quick look at the cat. "Talking of which it's not usual in France to feed cats fresh fish…?"

"It's not usual in England either."

She had two choices here, and she opted for the first. He could think what he liked about her being rich, but there was no way he was ever learning about the fish episode. She just wished Minou wouldn't keep brushing up against her leg. Although mostly reabsorbed, the bruise was still tender and obviously still very fishy.

She picked up her croissant for something to do. Pressing it against her mouth she heaved a silent sigh at the smell of warm bread as she allowed her lips to mould themselves to the familiar shape before biting into the warm crumbly pastry. Her eyes closed against the force of his stare even as her mind tried to think up something else to say but it was a complete blank. She could always resort to talking about the weather but that would be such a shame. There were so many things she wanted to know but didn't even have one word to start a conversation, any conversation.

Opening her eyes she was surprised at the expression on his face, quickly masked as he reached out for his own croissant. There was longing in that gaze, longing and something else. It was a look she hadn't been on the receiving end of for a very long time; since a child really. It was a look that started a cacophony of shivers racing up and down her spine. It was a look she wanted to hoard to herself like a greedy man offered a drink in the desert. It was a look she never wanted to forget.

He adored her? He couldn't, surely? But that's what it looked like as she struggled to keep her lips from pulling apart into a ruddy great grin.

"So your men then," she made a herculean effort to restart the conversation on a normal footing even though all she wanted to do was to hide away in a darkened room so she could mull over that look. Men didn't look at women like that, they just didn't.

Instead of escaping, instead of running away, she watched as his hand paused on the way to his mouth, his eyes now firmly fixed on the pile of crumbs on his plate. Now he'd been rumbled, she intended to watch him like a hawk so she could catch that look again. In fact, from this point forward, she was going to make it her life's mission. She couldn't quite stop a gentle smile from escaping her lips, her lungs fit to burst with happiness at the thought of being adored by someone; at the thought of being adored by him.

"Mmm?"

"Why, if you're an architect are you up there managing them? I thought you were a brickie or whatever the French call them."

"They're called brickies over here too. My manager is off sick at the moment so I decided to handle it myself."

"I see," although she didn't see at all. As an architect he should be spending his time designing, not wasting it overseeing his builds. Her mind scrolled back to what she'd learnt about him designing spectacular prize winning buildings, but perhaps this was his project, his baby.

"So the building opposite." She tipped her head to look up at him. "You're not just the architect then, you're…?"

"The owner you mean, or the mug that's sunk his whole life into creating a dream?" He pushed his mug away and folded his arms across his chest. "Yep, that would be me."

"Your dream," she repeated, parrot fashion.

"My dream, my vision. Call it what you like."

"But you're building apartments; flats like this one aren't you?" She waved a hand at the giant billboard pinned to the side of the building.

"Yes, and no. Apartments, specially designed apartments suitable for people with a range of both abilities and disabilities." His eyes narrowed. "Most apartments just cater for one type of person. You, and the other people here with you are all youngish professionals?"

"We have to be to cope with the stairs."

He laughed. "My apartments are innovative in that they're adapted for both able-bodied professionals, families and those with disabilities. All the doors are extra wide to accommodate both buggies and wheelchairs. All the kitchens are designed with adaptability in mind. All the sockets are at waist height; out of the reach of little fingers but also wheelchair accessible. All the balconies are reinforced glass, high enough to protect inquisitive toddlers, but still functional for wheelchair users."

Her smile broadened, her eyes never leaving his face. "Wow, bloody wow! How fantastic is that? I'll just bet investors are clamouring to jump on board."

"Again yes and no," the wry smile back. "Yes, because they can see the profit margins creeping up. But no, when they see what I intend to ask for, they disappear into the ether." He reached out and took her hand, examining her short well-kept nails free of varnish. "This isn't about making an exorbitant amount of money, Sarah. I'll never be a rich man," his eyes joining hers briefly. "It's about designing affordable adaptable housing that can in effect take the owner from birth to death without them ever having to move."

"Hence not replacing your project manager and bricklaying in your spare time?" she added softly.

"It's much better exercise than spending money on a gym I never had time to attend anyway." He met and held her gaze. "If you'd like, I can show you around?"

She interrupted, her eyes gleaming. "I'd love to see it."

"Okay, I'll tidy up here if you want to grab a jacket or something."

"What about food?"

"It's all taken care of. The only thing left is you and your bikini."

"So where are you taking me on this picnic then?" she asked, following him down the stairs.

She'd torn back into her bedroom and rummaged through her drawers for her bathers before adding sun cream and a straw hat for good measure. May might have nudged April out of the way for another year but sunrays were sneaky. With skin like hers she was only safe in the middle of a storm where every bit of sky was obliterated by cloud. Strawberry wasn't a good look on any day but especially not today, especially not with him.

Her eyes wandered over his springy dark brown hair to where it curled along the top of his collar while she waited for his answer. She wasn't one for long hair in men and any longer she'd be getting her scissors out. But he didn't give off the air of someone too bothered about his looks. It was more he just hadn't the time to go to the hairdresser. He'd thrown on a blue chambray shirt with sleeves pushed up to the elbows and, as her gaze lowered, she noted yet another pair of shorts which he appeared to live in unless he was out on the town. Part of her wondered if he wore them all year round even as another part managed to control her eyes long enough to shift them upwards away from his firm bum before he turned and caught her checking him out.

"I thought it was time I showed you my stately pile," he answered, pulling open the main door before letting her dip under his arm to sneak out first.

"Yeah right! If it's anything like my parents stately pile, I should have brought an extra cardigan," she replied, glancing down at her thick black woollen jacket. "My father is a real one for economising on heat and there are more drafts at Cosgrave Manor than in the average wind tunnel."

"Wait till you see mine." He commiserated, "It's not far, only about forty minutes or so."

"And you commute each day?"

"*D'accord*, unless I stay on-site. But curling up in a sleeping bag with only a stone floor for comfort isn't my idea of a good night's sleep."

Grabbing her hand he gave it a gentle squeeze before heading across the road.

"Come on, I'll show you the building first. There's still a lot to do but, now the roof's completed, we can start fitting it out."

He picked out a couple of hard hats from a pile in the corner before gently pushing one on top of her head. "Company rules I'm afraid," he added, dropping a kiss on her cheek. "It suits you."

Making their way through the wire security gates he took her through a maze of brick piles and machinery before reaching the entrance, which led into a large reception area, or what would be a large reception area when it was plastered and floored.

"We've finished on the outside now so the plumbers and electricians have taken over for the next few weeks," he said, pointing to the large hole in the ceiling where the lift was going. Taking her hand again, he directed her to the first door. "We've planned some ground floor apartments for those who'd prefer not to be upstairs. Of course they won't have balconies but they will have access to a small garden instead."

Looking around she was stunned at the open plan feeling of space that the cleverly designed apartment created. Stepping carefully to avoid the trenches for underfloor heating she skirted around the edge of the lounge to poke her head through the doors of the two smaller rooms complete with large ceiling to floor windows.

"The lounge faces south-west so it'll get the evening sun, but I've made both bedrooms north facing to capture the early morning light," his voice anxious.

"Can I put my name down now?"

He laughed and, swivelling her around in his arms placed a quick kiss on the tip of her nose.

"You like it then?"

"I love it," her face slightly pink. "It's…" She stepped back to spread both hands wide. "It's perfect."

In her mind's eye she could already see the plain white walls splattered with bright abstract prints. The concrete floor covered with ceramic tiles of earthenware hues. The modern open-plan kitchen separated from the living space with a breakfast bar and rich pine stools.

"With a kitchen area along the far wall," she added, gesturing to the corner. "And a large squidgy sofa positioned to watch the children playing in the garden…" She hadn't realised she'd expressed her thoughts out loud until he tweaked the end of her ponytail.

"I'm sorry, I got carried away."

"Oh, don't mind me," he said, throwing back his head with a laugh. "So how many children are you planning on having then?"

The colour on her face intensified as she said, "Me! I wasn't talking about me, and anyway I'm not planning on having any," she added, turning back towards the door, "shouldn't we be going?"

"Yes we should." He paused and then flung a casual arm across her shoulder as they made their way out of the building and over to his car.

Safely ensconced in the warm interior, she thought she'd escaped having to answer the question that was hanging over them like a thundercloud ever since he'd asked it. They'd talked about the empty streets and the chiming Sunday church bells and a hundred other topics but of course he was biding his time. He was waiting for the perfect opportunity to drop it back into the conversation like the proverbial brick.

They'd passed the deserted kindergarten school before he interrupted her halting discourse on the array of flowering mop head hydrangeas that seemed to grow with increasing regularity now they'd left the centre of Paris.

Placing his hand on her knee but with eyes fixed ahead he finally said. "That's a shame; you'd make a great mum."

"You don't know that."

"Oh I think I do, *ma petite*; the way you've already started to mother little *Minou*."

"There's a vast difference in taking on a cat to having full responsibility for a child."

"Not really, it's all about love and, from where I'm sitting you've got more than enough to share around," he said, throwing her a sideways look from narrowed eyes.

"Well it's a moot point anyway."

"What?"

"It's a moot point. In other words it's irrelevant, completely and utterly immaterial."

"Why? I thought it would be very relevant," his voice so soft she had to strain to hear him.

"Not if you've decided not to have them. My mother nearly died when she had me and things like that tend to run in families. I don't want to risk it, and I really don't want to talk about it anymore," she added, patting his hand absentmindedly as she turned her head to look out of the window.

She threw him a look as she tried to work out what had made her divulge something so central to who she was, even as she noticed the sudden whiteness around his jawline. She'd forgotten how embarrassed men got about such things and they were merely passing acquaintances after all. In a few weeks he'd move on to his next project and she'd be leaving Paris herself when her term came to an end. He'd probably dump her now anyway, she thought, a wry smile tugging at her lips. Who'd want to go out with her after they discovered that she was scared of getting pregnant? It was also one of the reasons marriage to Rupert, whilst unsavoury and unwanted, wasn't something completely out of the question. He'd already got four grown-up children from his first two marriages and was dead against any more.

He must have felt her eyes on him because; before she could turn away he'd touched her hand. "My home is just around the next corner…"

She'd expected him to pull up outside one of the small cottages that straggled the roadside of many a French country lane. Instead, she found herself being driven through a set of thick wrought-iron gates reminiscent of Cosgrave Manor. There was even a long swirling driveway disappearing out of sight behind a display of ornamental box trees. Just at its end she could see spiralling turrets stretching out towards the sky but that was all, the rest of the imposing building was hidden from view.

The gateway and entrance whilst as grand as her parents in both form and size had a distinctly neglected feel. The sand covered drive was sprouting more than the odd weed while the hedges were in urgent need of a good prune. Even the powerful gates looked as if they could do with a lick of paint, something Hopper oversaw with the zealous eye that bespoke both his position and worth.

Ignoring the drive, he pulled in behind the gatehouse, leaning across to open her door before collecting a large hamper from the boot. Once inside, he placed the basket in the kitchen before returning to where she was standing in the miniscule hall.

"What about I show you around and then that swim I promised?"

"I thought you were joking?"

"Really? I never joke." He smiled, tapping the end of her nose with his knuckle. "There's a swimming pool by the main house that I've managed to keep in usable condition. It's a great way to relax and chill after a day on site."

"I'll just bet it is." Her mind brimming with questions; questions she was pretty sure she'd soon find the answers to. He was a complete enigma; this tall, good-looking man, and she didn't want him to be. She wanted to know everything there was to know about him; after all he knew nearly everything about her, apart from her shoe size.

"So this is the lounge, as you can see." She followed him through the first door on the right, which opened into a bright west-facing room with views over a small, well-tended garden. Its plain white walls were in stark contrast to the old, blackened, wooden beams and mahogany-stained floorboards but the addition of a large sofa pushed up in front of the wood burner turned what could have ended looking like a doctor's waiting room into a comfortable home. There were a couple of newspapers on the stool and an open book turned upside down to mark his page. In fact, all that was missing was a cat, she thought with a smile as he grabbed her hand and pulled her into the kitchen.

"I only finished this a few weeks ago. What do you think?" His eyes were on her face as she took in the sleek black lines and granite surfaces. There was even a cat flap she noted with a smile, thinking suddenly of Minou and how much he'd love it here.

She arched an eyebrow. "How do you keep it so clean and tidy?"

"It helps if you don't use it much," he said on a laugh, opening the fridge to reveal a carton of milk and a few bottles of beer. Unbuckling the straps on the basket he took out a bottle of Muscadet and placed it in the special rack provided before turning back to her. "The bathroom's upstairs if you need to…"

"No, I'm fine, thanks." She perched on one of the bar stools hidden under a spare worktop.

"So how long have you lived here then, it's a gatehouse isn't it?" Her eyes focussed on the edge of the gate-post just visible from the window.

"That was a long time ago. I should get them removed but I quite like them, apart from the security. It's quite isolated around here even though it's only a stone's throw from Versailles."

He stood up and stretched, giving her a crooked smile. "I'm not used to such late nights." Holding out his hand he added. "Come on; let's see if some of this fresh air can wake me up, and what about that swim I promised?"

He left her in the hall only to return within seconds with a couple of large fluffy towels under one arm. "I hope you're hungry, *ma chérie*?" Flashing her a smile from under his brows even as his hand reached up to run a knuckle over her lower lip. "Apart from spicy chicken I was in the dark with what you like."

She felt her mouth tremble at his touch and saw his eyes lingering where his finger had only been seconds before. Biting down on her lip she turned away to pick up her bag. She could tell him what her tastes were, but she had an inkling he knew as the atmosphere suddenly changed from just two friends enjoying a peaceful Sunday outing to being charged with enough hidden emotion and desire to power Flamanville Nuclear Power Station.

"Oh damn it to hell."

"What?"

She found herself twisted back within his arms, her bag dropping to the floor with a bang, but she didn't hear the bang. All she heard was the thumping of her heart as he lifted up both hands to cradle her head. All she felt was his eyes as they scrolled over her face with that look again. All she saw was his mouth and then she closed her eyes as feelings and emotions took over.

Sarah had been kissed before. There was the stable hand, Angus. He'd pinned her against the wall of the barn on her sixteenth birthday, but the smell of sweaty horse flesh squashed any lingering memories of what was her first kiss. She remembered he'd limped for days after the well-aimed kick to his groin but at least that was the last time he'd ever come near her without a horse's lead in his hand.

Then there was Paul. Paul whom she'd thought special; maybe even the one. He'd smelt of beer and stale Indian, or Chinese, or whatever other fast food he'd lived on in the halls. In fact, his breath was the only reason she hadn't moved their goodnights into the bedroom: if his mouth was that bad what would the rest of him smell like?

Rupert, well she didn't want to think about Rupert: Rupert with his meaty hands and sweaty upper lip. Up until now she'd avoided anything over and above a kiss to the cheek, but the way his hands always managed to squeeze her in places she didn't want to be squeezed was a revelation, or should that be revulsion? They say always save the best til last and she knew as Pascal's lips touched hers that this wasn't just a kiss. This wasn't just the meeting of two young things eager to get it on. This was soul kissing.

There were no fireworks or explosions. There wasn't even the sound of ringing bells or trumpets heralding a new dawn. There was Sarah and Pascal falling irrevocably in love in his tiny hall somewhere near Versailles. The kiss, slow, sweet and lingering went on for seconds but felt like hours. His hands remained cradling her face, his fingertips intertwined in her hair, free now from the usual confines of its ponytail. Her hands, well she didn't know what to do with her hands so she let them hang by her side, wishing with all her heart she had the nerve to wrap them around his back in an effort to bring him closer.

Finally they pulled away, his hands moving from her face to the gentle slope of her shoulders before drawing her into a gentle hug. Her head filled that little dip just under his chin and after a moment she found the courage she'd been looking for and wrapped her arms around his back.

"Are you all right, *ma chérie*?" he whispered into her ear. "I wasn't expecting that to happen."

What could she say as she felt her heart settling down in her chest? She'd never been asked by a man if she was all right, well apart from her dad on the odd occasion he was actually around when she'd done something stupid like falling off her pony and breaking her arm.

Things were different now. Things were impossibly different from last night. Last night she'd finally decided to have a no-strings attached fling with this handsome man with *come to bed* eyes the colour of amber and muscles to die for. Apart from being the envy of all her friends she'd finally be able to lay to rest the photo of her all alone in that café. The photo that had turned her from an anonymous girl to someone the whole of the British public seemed to feel sorry for. There'd been letters innumerable in both the Times and the Telegraph about the difficulties young women faced away from their parents, and the potential damage in releasing details of her whereabouts to the battalion of fortune hunters.

It was only now she realised just how thankful she was to that cameraman. She hadn't been able to go back to her apartment just as her favourite café was now a stranger. Cara and her boyfriend had come to her rescue by collecting her belongings and letting her move into their lounge until she'd found her new apartment; the unusually vacant apartment that is until she realised its proximity to the building-site opposite.

What yesterday had been a fling, an exploration into her sexuality and what she might have been missing all these years was now something different. Now she was in love, impossibly, irrevocably in love with what her mother would term a bit of rough. Now she was lost because, no matter how wealthy or well educated he was, the barriers set in place by society meant that, whichever path she chose, would be a rocky one. Her grandmother would have understood, as would Aunty Popsy, but her mother would never understand. If she continued on her current journey she'd end up alienating almost everyone, apart from Cara and the Hoppers.

So no, she wasn't all right. She'd never be all right again. A fragment of a song, or was it a poem, suddenly popped out of nowhere, maybe Tennyson, she wasn't sure. "Better to have loved and lost than never to have loved at all." Was it? She didn't know.

Instead of replying she leant back and placed a soft kiss against his chin, the only place within reaching distance and changed the subject.

"Come on, let's go for that swim."

Chapter Five

12th May. I don't deserve to be called French. I'm a member of the most romantic nation in the world and yet I launched myself at her like a testosterone fuelled teenager. Where's my reserve, my planning, my strategy? There was none, only instinct and my instinct told me to kiss her. I'm lucky I wasn't slapped, more than lucky.

He felt her distance and knew he was the cause. He knew he shouldn't have kissed her; not like this, not here, not now. He should have wined her and dined her. There should have been flowers, lots of flowers and not just roses and orchids. Fresh bunches of sweet smelling lavender and stock; flowers like the ones that struggled to grow in his little patch of ground by the side of the house. He'd pick some for her later.

He wanted to woo her like some lovesick pup just out of short trousers because wasn't that just what he was? He'd fallen in love at first sight without even knowing her name, or who or what she was. He'd thought her French and then American until he'd finally realised if he ever met her he'd be playing with fire. He wasn't sure which one of his mates on site had pinned the photo up behind his desk with the *poor little rich girl* caption, and in truth he didn't care. They were good lads, all of them, happy to help with a day of grass cutting at the chateau. With good pay came loyalty, at least he hoped it did.

No, he shouldn't have kissed her. He shouldn't have been tempted to spend more time in her company but he couldn't seem to help himself. Their timelines had crossed and now seemed forever tangled, very much like the undoable knot he'd been forced to use on her robe. There was no way back for him now. There was no way back for him ever.

Picking up her bag, along with the towels, he grabbed her hand in his and, pulling the door closed, started the long walk up the driveway. He'd have liked to place his hand across her shoulders and hug her to his side, their hips banging gently like lovers but he didn't. He was well past the casual arm draping that came with friendship. He'd wanted to take her in his arms the first time he'd spotted her struggling out of that taxi all those weeks ago but, by the time he'd hauled himself down the side of the building she'd already disappeared into the apartment block. He'd remembered the ribbing from the building crew and had watched from afar; watched and waited for the ideal opportunity to introduce himself. Fate was on his side after weeks of inopportunity and he'd grabbed his moment with both hands.

Now, as the silence between them turned from comfortable to oppressive, he knew he'd blown it. He'd been too quick, too impulsive, too demanding and, if her expression was anything to go by, she was about to make him pay for it with her silence.

When she finally spoke her words were a surprise. "Are we gate-crashing, or trespassing or something? I don't really want to end up in gaol." She'd paused, pulling him to a stop, her free hand waving at the huge expanse of lawn interspersed with hydrangeas in need of a prune. "There's been enough in the papers…" she stuttered to a halt, her eyes shifting from his as she turned her head back to the gardens.

"No, we're not trespassing." He let go of her hand but only briefly so he could tilt her chin and look into her eyes. "Trust me, Sarah? I said I wouldn't do anything to hurt you last night, and that includes getting you arrested." He managed a laugh before pointing at the bend in the drive. "You'll see as soon as we get to the corner."

* * *

The driveway veered off to the left before twisting back on itself to reveal a large turreted chateau. Something clicked in her memory about turrets as she counted them; eight. Who the hell built a chateau with eight turrets? They only had two at Cosgrave Manor, two too many if Hopper was to be believed with all those spiral staircases to keep clean, not that he ever yielded as much as a feather duster or hoover. It was the army of women employed by the National Trust that came in on a daily basis to ensure not even the smallest dust mote remained.

They were facing the front entrance now, her eyes drawn to the large impressive studded door guarded by a pair of Baroque porticos more suited to an Italian villa than a French country residence. Her gaze flickered across to the many similarly ornate windows expecting to see movement; the edge of a curtain, a picture or two, a face. But all was silent, empty even or should that be eerie?

Letting go of his hand, she moved away to peer across at the sandstone frontage. "I don't get it," her eyes narrowing. "It doesn't make sense. Who owns…?"

"I do." He grimaced before grabbing her hand again. "Come on, I'll show you the rest."

He pulled her gently around the back to where *"the rest"* of the chateau should have been. The rest was a shock.

She'd been expecting more of the same. Instead there was crumbling fire blackened walls and collapsed wooden beams reminiscent of something out of a Jane Eyre movie finale.

He squeezed her hand, his eyes wandering over the charred remains of what should have been his home.

"There was a fire," his laugh dry now. "Of course there was a fire. I was away at Cambridge when I got the call. My uncle lived here on his own, with just his nurse and some servants to keep an eye on him. He was in a wheelchair by then, crippled with arthritis but still managing to get around, still managing his own affairs to a fashion; still a stubborn old Frenchman reluctant to take help when it was offered."

He dropped to the ground and pulled her beside him his fingers still linked in hers. "He'd taken me in after my parents' plane crash. He was all I knew really, all the family I had, and I was all the family he had." His eyes now back on the rubble. "They never worked out how the fire started but he used to smoke so it was probably that. All the servants escaped but they couldn't get to him." His voice trailed off to nothing and silence surrounded them like the aftermath of a wake, a silence more difficult to breach than the by-product of any kiss.

Sitting there holding hands she didn't know what to say. He'd lost everything; his parents first and now this.

There was nothing left other than the two of them staring at the wreckage of his life, and yet he was still trying to carry on with his dream, despite or because of the fire? Suddenly she had to know.

"Surely it can be rebuilt, brought back to its former glory. What about insurance?"

"He'd let things slip, *ma chérie*. I should have noticed. I should have been there to help but I was off gallivanting at university."

"But that's what he would have wanted. He'd have wanted you to make the most of yourself?"

"It didn't help him in the long run though, did it? He died alone in that upstairs room he refused to leave because of the memories it held. They couldn't get to him because he was a silly old man too wrapped up in the memory of his wife."

"But don't you see he wanted to be where he was happiest?"

She watched his face as she tried to think of something else to say to break the sadness that layered itself around them like a thick fog obliterating the sun. She had to think of something positive, something to change the mood back to what it had been. But there was nothing positive to be garnered from such a tragedy, only sadness.

She'd thought her life a misery, saddled as she was with the never ending pressure of not knowing who to trust, but at least she'd had a good childhood. No one knew more than her about the imperfections of her parents, wrapped up as they were in their own sense of personal wealth and importance. Nevertheless she'd been loved and taken care of. If it wasn't for that stupid *will* the world would have been hers for the taking.

She blushed now at how selfish she'd been; how selfish she still was. Here was a man who'd lost everything. Yet he'd still managed to crawl out from all that devastation to make something positive out of his life. He didn't moan at the injustices sent his way. He just got on with it.

Feeling tears prick the back of her eyes was the only encouragement she needed to change the sudden sad tempo. If she didn't move she'd be crying like a toddler who'd just lost the top off his ice-cream and that would never do.

"So where's this pool you were promising me then?" she said, pulling him to his feet with a mighty yank even though it felt like she was trying to shift a boulder.

He dragged his hands across his face briefly before lifting up her bag. "Good idea," his hand again reaching for hers. "There are far too many ghosts roaming about today for a poor French builder."

The soft golden water in an oasis of greenery was like a little bit of heaven after the oppression and memories of moments before. She knew it would be cold, but she didn't care. After all, they had an outdoor pool back at Cosgrave Manor so she was used to it.

"Hey, that's cheating!" he muttered, watching as she pulled off her top to reveal a simple black racing Speedo swimsuit. "I thought I said a bikini? What's this with you Brits and one pieces anyway? If us blokes had our way they'd be banned," he continued, moaning under his breath as he unbuttoned his shirt.

"It's not your lucky day, Pascal." Her eyes careful to avoid the large expanse of washboard stomach now he'd thrown his shirt alongside her top.

Oh God, he was beautiful, too beautiful to feast her eyes on. Instead of staring with her jaw dropped to her knees, she raced to the edge before executing a perfect dive, her body hardly causing a ripple as it punched through water. She felt rather than heard him follow, his arms slicing through the air like an Olympian. They met at the far end, their hands holding onto the side of the blue tiled edge.

"When I mentioned a swim, I didn't think you'd be a champion diver or anything?"

"I'm not; I'm just an enthusiastic amateur." She caught sight of the smile pulling at his lips as she listened to the way her words sounded and blushed. "Race you." She did a quick tumble turn and was off like a rocket only to find him waiting with arms folded at the other end.

"So what took you so long?"

Treading water while she caught her breath was the wrong thing to do as it meant she took her eyes off him for a second, but a second was long enough. Before she knew it he'd grasped her around the waist and plunged her deep into the water.

"Hey," she spluttered, as she broke through the surface with water streaming down her face.

"All's fair in love and war," his arms lingering around her waist, his fingers spanning the skin on her back setting up little tingles of anticipation across her body. Their eyes locked and, lifting her arms across his shoulders she joined her lips to his, eager suddenly to feel the pressure of skin against skin. As the kiss deepened, she wrapped her legs around his back, keen to increase the pace and pressure of his touch.

She never wanted this to end but end it did and at his hand. If it had been up to her they'd have stayed sandwiched up together for the rest of the afternoon.

He lessened his grip and, staring down at her flushed face, gently lowered her back into the water.

"We need to stop, Sarah," wrenching his hand through his hair.

"Why do we need to stop?" she paused, her look changing from loving to suspicious in an instant. "You're not married are you?"

"Me?" He let out a loud laugh scaring the birds in the trees. "Sarah, if I was married, believe me, I wouldn't be here."

"That doesn't stop most men from at least looking…"

"Well, I'm not most men."

"So, why do we need to stop then?" she replied, levering herself out of the pool. But the only answer she got was his silence.

She'd just discovered how much it hurt to be rejected and she didn't like it one little bit. There must be a reason for his rejection, but for the life of her she couldn't think what it might be. But, bending down for a towel before starting to dry her hair, she promised that before the day was out she'd make him tell her.

"Here, let me do that, I don't want you getting cold." He wrapped the spare towel around her shoulders and taking the other raised his hands to her head.

"Such long hair…"

"It's to make up for the boring mouse colour."

"Mice are pretty little things, small and delicate," he added, his eyes wandering down only to stop at the ugly mark on her leg.

"My god, you're hurt." He knelt on the grass and ran a gentle hand over the bruise.

"It's nothing, really. I just walked into a chair yesterday."

"What am I going to do with you, *ma petite*? First you bang your head, not forgetting your ankle and now this."

"As I said, its nothing." She grabbed her jeans and started pulling them on, keen to return the conversation back to his behaviour in the pool,

"You didn't answer my question, Pascal. What's the problem? We're both young, free and single." She wasn't about to let him off the hook without a fight. She felt like someone had just stolen all her Christmas presents from under the tree.

"None of us are free," his gaze not quite meeting hers as he fastened his shirt buttons with undue care.

"What, you're telling me you've got a girlfriend, or you're engaged?" She threw him a look laden with suspicion.

"Sarah, I wasn't talking about me. I was talking about you. What about this Rupert chap? What about this inheritance thing?" He grabbed her shoulders, his fingers instinctively curving in the gentlest of caresses. "Perhaps this was a bad idea, perhaps we should just go back…"

"No you don't." Her gaze steely. "You promised to feed me and I'm keeping you to it."

"Okay, but no more launching yourself at me, I only have so much willpower."

"You started it!"

"Yes, and now I wish I hadn't." He grabbed her hand and then the rest of their belongings before heading back to the gatehouse.

And now I wish I hadn't

The words reverberated around her head filling her mind with an array of thoughts. Why, what was wrong with her? Was it because she was clumsy, or perhaps inexperienced? Was it wrong to reach out to him in the pool, after all a woman knew when a man fancied her? Why else had he asked her on a date? Was it even a date? Maybe he just wanted to be friends?

Backwards and forwards her thoughts went as she tried to make sense of it all.

Now she knew about the chateau and a little more about him she'd started to allow dreams to fill her mind, tentative dreams where the chateau was miraculously restored to its former glory; dreams where her parents happily consented to her marriage to this would-be builder-landowner. He obviously had an impeccable background, which was all that interested her parents for; despite not needing their consent, she wanted it all the same.

Staring up into the cloudless sky, she couldn't believe how her hopes had come full circle. After Paul she'd given up on ideas of love and marriage. She'd long given up on the idea of filling her house with the sound of children's laughter. But now she'd allowed that dream back to invade her heart, and he'd burst it like a bubble. There was something he wasn't telling her, she just wasn't sure what.

They'd arrived back at the gatehouse and she watched as he carried out the basket before setting it on the large tartan blanket he'd thrown across the centre of the lawn.

"You were right about the amount of food." Her eyes glued to the basket as he pulled out smoked salmon parcels, hard-boiled eggs and numerous pots of assorted salads, not to mention a full quiche lorraine. There was even a box full of Buffalo wings, which he offered her with a smile.

Plates loaded they rested back on the cushions he'd pinched from the sofa as they sampled a little of everything.

Stretching out on the rug, her hand rested on her arm as she stared up at him. "That was gorgeous; I won't be able to eat for a week."

"What, no room for coffee and a *chocolat religieuse*?"

She sat up quickly, squinting across at him. "You haven't? Those funny little shoe bun men covered in…"

"*Chocolat, ma chérie*?" His eyebrows shot up.

Throwing a cushion at him she leant back again with a smile. "I always have room for *chocolat, ma chérie*," echoing his words. "But first a little siesta," she added, closing her eyes against the force of his gaze.

She'd only closed her eyes to get away from him and get back to her thoughts, but the rich food and wine at lunchtime on top of a late night worked their magic and soon enough she'd fallen into a deep sleep.

She woke with a start, unsure of where she was to find her eyes staring up at deep heavy clouds where before there had only been clear blue sky. She wasn't scared just puzzled as the morning unfolded before her and she remembered those kisses, kisses she'd hug to her for as long as she lived.

Turning she found Pascal asleep and, propping herself up on an elbow she examined his face. The faint lines across his forehead and around his eyes smoothed, giving her an inkling of the boy he'd once been before the strain of the past few years had clearly etched their mark on his skin. His hair was tousled, and she longed to reach out and smooth it straight but he wouldn't want that. He wanted nothing from her other than perhaps the odd kiss between friends. Her eyes scrolled down his body before returning back to his face only to find his eyes upon her. He lifted a sleepy hand and brushed her hair off her forehead where it hung like a curtain before curling his hand around her face.

"You're beautiful, Sarah, so beautiful."

She laughed, unsure of what to say. She'd never been called beautiful before. Pretty at a push after a visit to the hairdresser and dressed up to the nines but far from beautiful. She eyed her rumpled clothes and ratty hair, a smile hovering as she remembered the look she'd spotted on his face earlier. If he didn't want sex, then perhaps she could trust herself to believe his words. After all, if he truly adored her, he'd probably not see the lack of make-up and mound of freckles that were sure to have taken over her nose like a military invasion.

"You have freckles, I hadn't noticed before."

There, she just knew she should have worn her hat. Pulling away from his hand she sat up and poked him in the shoulder. "What about that cake you promised me, not to mention the coffee? This falling asleep on the job just won't do, you know."

"Slave driver," he grumbled, but stood to his feet all the same before pulling her up, their hands still linked.

"Sarah about before…"

But she interrupted with a little shush. "Pascal, we've had a lovely day. Let's leave it at that. I'm just going to pop upstairs."

"First door on the right."

She was a woman and snooping was second nature. In fact, just like her mother, she had a degree in nosiness and a diploma in curiosity, not that you'd ever get her to admit to being anything like her mother.

After washing her hands she made her way across the excuse of a landing before peering into the master bedroom. This time he'd chosen a bright sunny yellow for the north facing room, but looking out of the window at the glorious French countryside she could fully understand why he'd chosen it. The furniture was minimalist at best; the only thing filling the room was a large bed. There were no knickknacks or pictures; there was nothing to tell her anything more about him except that he was tidy and that he liked a big bed, her eyes transfixed to the plain virginal white cover.

Her mind worked overtime as she imagined just how many girlfriends he'd tested the springs on, even one being one too many. It was none of her business. Her gaze focussed on the slight head shaped indent on the pillow. It was none of her business and yet all of her business she thought on a sigh, finally backing out of the room. Thoughts like that only lead to unhappiness. She had no hold on him, and yet she was his. She was his completely, utterly, entirely. He didn't even need to ask.

Pushing the door open on the second bedroom was more of a surprise. Expecting either an unfinished room or an impersonal guest bedroom the bright office was a shock. Looking across at his work board she expected to find a drawing, but all that was pinned to the centre was a blank piece of paper. The rest of the office space was filled to the gills with wall to floor built-in bookcases stacked high with books and drawings and, also devoid of any personal touches. It could be any architects office anywhere apart from the view out of the window.

"So what did you get up to over the weekend then? I've been trying to phone you for what seems like days to find out what happened on Friday night with your parents."

Cara's voice broke into her reverie as she munched through her lunchtime baguette stuffed full of Camembert and blush red tomatoes. Moving up the bench to make room, she finished chewing before smiling at her friend. "Oh, you know just out and about with a certain French builder."

"Sarah, you didn't?" Cara's hand grasped hers, pinning both it and the baguette to the table with fingers made strong from all her piano practicing.

Lady Sarah and Lady Cara, more like sisters than best-friends had grown up on neighbouring estates and had even wrangled being sent to the same boarding school and then the same university where they'd both excelled in their instruments of choice. But where Sarah was happy to bumble along with perhaps a career in teaching, Cara was already set for stardom with concert recitals and even the odd television appearance.

"Not so loud." She threw a quick look over her shoulder, checking no one was within hearing distance. "I managed to persuade him to come and have dinner with my parents, the one problem being they'd brought Rupert along."

"What, that creep?" she sighed. "Why they still keep trying to fling him at you, I'll never know."

"They were trying to whittle me down, they very nearly managed." She split her baguette in two and passed the other half over with a smile. "He's not really a builder you know. He's this amazing architect with a head full of ideas to develop the most amazing apartments with people's needs at the heart of his designs," her eyes staring out over the little patio that bordered onto the cafeteria. "A bit like the NHS, but property instead of healthcare, from cradle to the grave."

"Not such a great idea then. We all know how much difficulty the NHS is in. It's all very well being noble, Sarah but who'll pay for the nanny?"

"I'm not going to marry him, and even if I was I wouldn't employ a nanny. I'd want to be there. Wouldn't you?"

She'd never confided in Cara about her fears over motherhood, which made her disclosure to Pascal all the more surprising.

But now wasn't the time or the place for confidences.

"Mmm, that's all very well, but what about at 3 am when they have colic or some other bratty ailment?"

Sarah eyed her across the top of her roll. "I do think you're running away a little from the point in hand. I've been out with him twice, well actually three times…"

"What, since Friday?" Cara's mouth dropped open. "So that means Friday, Saturday and Sunday dates does it?" She giggled. "God, I knew when you finally fell it would be bad but give the poor man a break. You must have worn him out. So when are you seeing him again then?"

"Tonight, I said I'd cook supper. It's to repay him back for yesterday and he does only work across the road," she qualified, her chin lifting in defiance.

"Of course he does." She reached out and patted her hand. "Just be careful, hun. You're not as experienced as me and men can be sneaky. He'll have you tied to the bedhead with a pile of dirty dishes in the sink and a pile of ironing in the basket before you know it."

Sarah changed the subject as an image scrolled across her consciousness of waking up next to him every morning for the rest of her life. She wouldn't mind about the dishes and the housework if she could have him by her side, but that was only a pipedream.

They'd barely spoken on the way back. The weather had finally let them down and he'd needed all his attention for the rain drenched roads, or at least that's what he'd told her. There was so much left unsaid, so many questions still left unanswered. She wanted to know his plans, all of them. She wanted to ask why he hadn't sold the estate and moved on. All that land was ripe for development being as it was so close to Versailles. He'd sell it in no time and use the money on his latest project instead of having to get investors in, but he wasn't going to tell her. Instead all she got was the most evasive of answers imaginable. They'd stopped off to pick up some flowers for her cat-loving neighbour *Madame Du Pont* but it was almost as if, now their day was over, he couldn't get away from her fast enough. There was no repeat of the heavy, heart thumping kiss of earlier, only a brotherly pat on the back and an almost reluctant promise to pop by after work to check on how Minou was settling in. He obviously had something on his mind, something he wasn't prepared to share with her so she'd let him go with a shy smile. She'd made up the bit about supper, but there'd be food ready all the same.

Wiping her mouth on a napkin she turned the conversation back to Cara's favourite topic. "So, where's your boyfriend then, I thought he'd be joining you for lunch?"

Cara had only been here a month when she'd met and fallen in love with Aaron, as talented with the violin as she was on the piano. Sarah wouldn't be surprised if she announced one day that they'd run off to get married, but then again, Cara was different. She'd never let her parents dictate what was right or wrong for her, not that they'd have objected to Aaron, the much-loved son of a wealthy Swiss hotelier.

"No such luck. He's practicing for a recital later and, as you know, music comes first."

"As if! He'd give it all up tomorrow if you asked him." They grinned at each other, secure in the knowledge that at least one of them had found their soul mate.

"So, what about grabbing a coffee on the way home if I can't entice you away from the kitchen?" Cara asked with a smile. "My treat for letting me share your lunch."

"I can't." She rolled her eyes. "I haven't told you about Minou yet."

"Minou? Kitty? You haven't gone and got yourself a little kitty? "she said, clapping her hands together. "Well I'll just have to pop along to see it, I adore…"

"You won't adore this one! Minou isn't a kitten as such," her mind recalling his scrawny body and uneasy gaze. "More of a street urchin in need of a better hand than life has currently dealt him."

"Well, he'll get that," she exclaimed with a smile. "You were always picking up strays when you were little and spoiling them rotten. There was even that nickname they gave you in school, what was it again? Oh yeah, I remember. Soft-touch Sarah."

"Don't remind me," her head in her hands.

"It's nothing to be ashamed of. You just have a greater capacity to love than almost anyone I know."

"You're the second person that's told me that recently," she said, lifting her head. "It hasn't got me very far though has it? You're the one with the soul mate while I…while all I have is a scabby cat."

"But I don't understand? What about that builder?"

"Pascal? I think he's started to go off me already. He almost dumped me at the door last night. He wouldn't even come in for a coffee."

"Oh, Sarah," holding her hand.

"Don't worry about me, Cara," her eyes glinting. "I was always planning a career up north, perhaps teaching at some kind of girl's school with my cat for company and, now I have the cat, I'm halfway there."

"Here's the post *patron,* I'm just nipping out to buy some croissants for the lads if you want one?" Rexi's eyes landed on the rolled up sleeping bag in the corner with a frown. "*Mon Dieu,* you didn't sleep up here again last night when you have that lovely…"

"Fell asleep at my desk," throwing him a rueful smile, one hand rubbing the back of his neck. "When I woke up, I'd glued my face to that brochure on bathroom fittings the plumber dropped off last week."

"I'll be getting you a double expresso."

"Here." He threw him his wallet. "It's on me."

"What, trusting me with all that lolly."

"If you can find any, you'll be lucky." He waved a hand towards the door. "Off with you, and leave me with trying to find someone to fund the rest of this *blanc éléphant.*"

Leafing through the post, he quickly separated it into piles. There were more catalogues like the one he'd had to peel from his cheek earlier and then the thick heavy envelopes which screamed of financial institutions. The first and most important was confirmation of funding for the next part of the build. It came at a cost; one he had little choice of accepting. He'd have to sign away 49% of the ownership. But he'd still retain the key 51% and that was all that mattered.

Apartment Plaisant along the Rue Fountain was only the first of the many similarly styled properties he hoped to develop and, providing there was money in the bank for the next one, he'd be happy. His hand stilled on the letter because that wasn't quite true anymore, not now. To be truthful it wasn't true at all. He'd be lying to himself if he wouldn't give it up if she asked him to.

Placing the envelope in his top drawer for later, his fingers tore through the remaining letters in seconds. Another offer for the cottage, this time nearly twice its worth, which he screwed up into a ball before aiming it at the bin in the corner. Over his dead body!

His uncle, for all his peculiar ways had willed the cottage to him within a year of losing his parents. There was a letter to accompany the bequest and the hope that he wouldn't ever feel the necessity to sell it on. Chateau Sauvarin was his home for as long as he wanted it to be. Pascal's eyes followed the screwed up letter that had missed the bin by miles. They'd have to drag him out of the cottage kicking and screaming. His plan had always been to stay there. He was a man of simple needs. Providing he had a bed to sleep on and room for his work board, he'd manage.

He'd even drawn up tentative plans for an extension if he ended up a family man in need of additional bedrooms, but now…

Scattering the remainder of the post across the desk he rested his head in his hands. But now it looked like he wasn't going to be a father unless they chose to adopt. It had been his greatest hope that, when he eventually met the girl of his dreams, they'd spend long happy hours under the duvet filling the nursery to capacity. He wouldn't let any child of his have the isolated lonely existence he'd had to suffer. Without the intervention of his uncle, he'd have ended up in an orphanage so he counted himself one of the lucky ones, lonely but lucky, that is until Sarah had come along. Now he didn't know what to think.

He knew she fancied him. He wasn't conceited. He didn't have the time or the inclination to do more than run his hands through his hair in lieu of a comb but he knew he was attractive to women. He could have pretty much any woman he looked at, and even if he wasn't looking, they plonked themselves in front of his path to trip over. He smiled, remembering the way she'd wrapped her legs around his waist: the feel of her smooth wet skin under his palms as he'd restrained himself from touching any part of her other than her shoulders, her face, her neck, her lips. Squeezing his eyes shut he tried and failed to erase that image of her in the water.

Her fancying him wasn't going to be enough. He loved her to distraction. He'd do anything and everything for her at the moment except perhaps sleep with her, his hands scrubbing across his stubble. If he slept with her; if he plunged himself into her, body and soul, he'd never recover. He'd drown from an overload of thought, feeling and deed. No, he wouldn't drown he'd be extinguished by the flame of desire that threatened to engulf him, and he was only sitting at his desk!

He wouldn't, he couldn't sleep with her, not if he was to make any sense of this insanity that had occupied his soul ever since he'd first laid eyes on her. He was lost without her. He'd be inconsolable after her, and then what? Work wasn't the answer. What would be?

Chapter Six

13th May. All I want is Pascal and I get Rupert. He doesn't come bearing gifts, unless you can call a sliced white a gift. He doesn't bring anything except disaster.

"You're making a huge mistake, Sarah." He tried to grab her hand, but she managed to hide it behind her back just in time.

Rupert had accosted her outside her building and frog-marched her up the stairs where he'd demanded a sandwich, having missed his lunch. He'd even had the foresight to bring his own sliced loaf, a sacrilege in France.

"I'm not eating any of that baguette rubbish," he'd said, slapping the bag on the counter. "What's that flea-bitten rat doing here?" putting out a foot to kick Minou as he entwined himself around Sarah's leg.

"That's my cat, and I've yet to de-flea, or indeed worm him so I wouldn't be so keen to touch him," she added, noting with a smile the way he pulled back out of the kitchen with a look of disgust.

Pushing her hair off her face she listened with one ear to the coffee maker while she tuned back into the conversation.

"In what way Rupert?"

"He's only after your money, you know."

"What, and you're not?"

She watched him, but there was no visible sign of a reaction apart from the slight tightening of his jawline where flab merged with the first of his many necks.

"Well, of course I'm not." He laughed. "I know I'm a little older than you…"

"By twenty seven years."

He ignored that. "With age comes experience…"

"Along with a couple of ex-wives and four kids. Just remind me how much she managed to squeeze out of you again; eight million wasn't it?"

"Sarah, your parents are happy…"

"Don't bring my parents into this; in fact please don't mention them. You may be able to smarm your way into their lives and hang onto their coat-tails like a little puppy but that's nothing to do with me."

The coffee machine finished its last gurgle and she almost ran back to the kitchen to make his sandwich. If only she had the nerve, she'd throw the ham into Minou's bowl and give him cheese instead. So what if he was lactose intolerant? It wasn't her problem if he spent the rest of the day in search of the nearest loo.

But Minou, sound asleep on top of Rupert's sliced white had beaten her to it. With one lazy eye half closed in a sort of hairy grey wink she could almost be excused into thinking it was on purpose after that badly aimed kick. Surely cats weren't that intelligent? The Hoppers's ginger tom spent all his time asleep in front of the Aga, only deigning to jump down off his rocking chair when someone opened up a tin of cat food.

She plonked his peculiarly shaped doorstep ham and mayo on the table before returning with a tray of coffee. In truth, she felt like a drink but coffee would have to do. She'd need her wits about her with wily Rupert on the prowl.

He sat back after munching his way through his belated lunch at top speed, hands gently folded on his lap as he exuded the image of the veritable banker he was.

"Mmm, I have to say that was the best sandwich I've had in years. There seemed to be an added piquancy to the bread. I must buy some to take home," patting his stomach with a sigh.

She struggled to contain her laughter, but inside she was in fits of giggles while he sat there with that smarmy look glued to his face. Nothing fazed him. He could have been in the middle of a shareholder meeting for all the emotion he showed. She knew he despised her. He despised her for the power she had, and if she were foolish enough to become engaged to him, all that would go. She often wondered why Aunt Popsy had decided on engaged rather than married before she could inherit. As a staunch feminist she'd balked at giving all that initial power out of the family. She'd probably predicted fortune hunters would be out in droves and this was her way of hopefully stopping them. Sarah would inherit with no one else having legal entitlement if she decided not to go through with the wedding.

"You do know you're a laughing stock?"

She'd just taken a sip of hot coffee and nearly choked on it. Continuing to swallow she forced herself to settle her cup back on its china saucer before looking him straight in the eye.

"Excuse me?"

"You're a laughing stock, Lady Sarah." The way he pronounced the Lady part, more of an insult than an honour. "Your behaviour on Saturday night was disgusting. Fancy allowing a Frog to put his finger in your…"

"How did you…?" Her eyes wide. "Were you following me? How dare you!" She leapt out of her chair, splattering coffee over the table.

"Sit down." He ordered and only continued speaking when she was perched back on the edge of her seat.

"And then yesterday," he continued, his eyes flint. "Sex in the pool; how very common," he said, shaking an envelope out to reveal an array of close-ups of Pascal and her in a variety of positions: in the pool kissing, asleep together on the rug in his garden.

"You had me followed. Unbelievable! If my money's that important to you, have it, take the lot."

"If that's a marriage proposal I accept."

"It wasn't." Her eyes still pinned to the table as she stood up for a second time, only to sit down again as his arm flicked out and grabbed her wrist.

"I'm only protecting you, my dear. He's a fortune hunter; everyone in Paris knows he hasn't got two Euros' to rub together. They're about to foreclose on his build and his last investor will be pulling out as of tomorrow."

She looked up from massaging her arm and the ugly red finger marks already appearing on her skin. "What, unless I agree to be your wife?"

"You catch on quick, my dear."

She stood up, scraping the legs of her chair back against the floor.

"You disgust me." She smiled, suddenly remembering yesterday. "He can always sell the chateau."

"I'm afraid not. He'd need to own it first."

She frowned. Surely that couldn't be right. She was sure he'd said he owned it. But if he'd lied about that what else had he lied about: the tie, university, the adoring look? She shook her head, trying to clear all the negative vibes Rupert was willing her way. "He told me he…"

"That's true enough. He does own it, but only in his life time." His eyes staring her out like a cat toying with a mouse. "It's willed to his offspring, not him."

Offspring he'll never have if he hitches himself to her star, she reminded herself as what little colour faded from her face.

"What about the cottage? Surely with all the work he's done…"

"Oh, he owns the cottage all right, but some poky two up two down in the heart of the country isn't going to bring the kind of money he needs. We're talking millions here not pennies." He arched his fingers together, his lazy smile not reaching his eyes. "What he needs is the support from someone high up in the financial world to put a good word in for him."

"What? Like you?"

"How did you ever guess," his voice sarcastic. "But I'll only help him if…"

"What you mean is you won't interfere with the loans he's already been granted unless I agree to your terms?"

"Why so clinical, Sarah? After all, marriage is a partnership and I do worship the ground under your feet."

"So you'd marry me if I decided to give all the money away then?"

"Er no, what would be the point of that, my dear." He started fiddling with his cuff links. "Charities like that have more than enough without needing our hard earned money."

"I'm surprised you have the decency to include me, it's not as if I'll see any of it." She met his eyes squarely. "So just how much debt are you in Rupert?"

"No need to worry your pretty little head about me, my dear. You'll be well provided for. All you need to do is accept my proposal so I can announce it to the world as per that stupid codicil…"

She felt the breath leave her body as she finally realised he had her trapped. If she didn't agree to marry him Pascal would lose everything; everything except his white elephant inheritance, which would hang around his neck like one of Marley's chains to remind him of everything he'd lost.

Feeling the pressure of tears build up was the last piece in the puzzle. Why on earth should she feel upset about someone she didn't even know?

But she did know him; a tiny voice screamed over and over, the crescendo exploding in her ears. She loved him completely and utterly and not just him, everything about him from his unruly hair to his oh so sexy voice. She loved him and everything he was trying to do with his life in an effort to make sense out of his miserable past. She loved him and he'd never know because to stay and tell him would mean disaster. Rupert held both of their futures in the palm of his clammy hands and there was nothing she could think of to change that.

She'd have to marry him, she finally decided just as one tear tipped over and, balancing on her lower eyelash, gently dropped on to her cheek. If Aunty Popsy wasn't already dead for putting her in such a position, she'd happily murder her.

Placing both hands on the table she met his eyes. "Do you know just how much I loathe you?"

"Probably. So do I take it we're engaged?"

She didn't wait for the evening. She didn't go to the poissonnerie to buy oysters to accompany the champagne already cooling in the fridge. She didn't throw more than a passing glance towards the stockings she'd laid on top of her freshly made bed. Stockings and her dressing gown as he seemed to like it so much; nothing else would be needed in the art of seducing her Frenchman.

Instead she left the apartment in a rush and headed to the building site. The men were just leaving, their eyes wide at the sight of a woman, any woman daring to breach their very male domain. They were friendly enough once they knew she was here to see Pascal and the cheeky one, the one that always waved and wolf-whistled the loudest, pressed his hard hat on her head and, pointing towards the office whispered in her ear before joining his mates at the entrance,

"Go gently on him luv, he's had a bit of a shock."

I'll bet he has, she thought, offering him the briefest of thanks before watching him race ahead to join his mates, even now pole hopping down the metal rods instead of taking the stairs.

She managed to swallow the hard lump that had invaded the back of her throat at the sight of Rupert rubbing his hands together like an excited six year old. She'd closed the door on him with a sharp snap having also managed to avoid his greedy mouth with a quick twist of her head.

Once they were married, it would be a different story. She'd need more than quick reflexes and a bedroom lock to repel his advances. That was something she'd have to think about, but not now. Now she had to say a forever goodbye; a forever goodbye to Pascal, to Paris, to her future for, as sure as night followed day, her life was over.

Both hands gripped the round door handle as she leant her forehead against the cool metal and prayed with all her might for help to get her through the next few minutes.

She wasn't a religious person. Christmas, weddings, baptisms and funeral attendance was about the sum of her devotion. It wasn't that she didn't care, in truth she'd never given that side of life much thought. For her mother, religion was an excuse to buy a new hat. For her father, an opportunity to display the new car. For her it was just something she did when duty dictated, but now she prayed; she prayed like never before.

She found him with his head in his hands, an untouched cup of coffee left to grow cold by his side and she knew before he said anything. She knew Rupert had been up to his tricks and had somehow managed to stop his loan, just as she knew how he felt. He felt exactly how she felt. He felt as if he'd just lost everything.

Her eyes scrolled around the office taking in the expected glamour girl calendar just visible under his jacket; his jacket all but obliterating everything except for part of a foot and half a breast. Her gaze shifted and then paused, her heart plummeting deep within her chest because there too was her face staring back at her. Her face ripped out from the newspaper and pinned above his desk; the words echoing and reverberating around the silent room like a ghostly serenade.

Poor little rich girl and her sax.

Would those words haunt her forever?

She must have made a sound then, a groan maybe because now, instead of staring at the top of his head, she was staring right into his eyes. He looked as if he hadn't slept, the shadows under his eyes deep bruises pressed into his skin, his face pale under his tan.

Words dragged from her mouth, words from the heart.

"How could you," her gaze flickering to the cutting behind his head. "I thought you were different but you're just like the rest of them. You were only after my money and I let you..."

And I let you into my heart, but she didn't finish the sentence.

She felt bile build up in her throat as tears pressed against her eyelids. She couldn't bear it. She couldn't bear for Rupert to be right but the evidence was right there in front of her. She knew the truth, and the truth hurt.

Heaving a breath she knew she'd explode if she didn't escape; the small office suddenly a prison, the stale smell of coffee mixed with male heat making her dizzy.

She felt rather than saw him rush from his seat to help her into the spare chair.

"Here, sit down…"

But she shook him away as she concentrated on gulping air into her lungs. She had to leave. She had to escape the office. She had to escape him before she said or did something she'd regret. But her legs suddenly wouldn't take her weight. It took all her powers of concentration to sink down on the chair, her anger deserting her to leave behind only desolation and loneliness. She had to leave, but first she had to know why, her eyes finally meeting his. She knew why, but she needed to hear the words come out of his lips and then she'd leave.

"Just tell me why, Pascal? Why me? Why not someone else?"

"It's not what you think…"

"Well then, tell me what it is because from where I'm sitting it looks exactly like that." Her eyes back on the photo.

She watched him brush his hands across his face, his eyes following hers.

"The picture was a joke."

"A joke?"

She would have stood up except for the hand on her shoulder gently pushing her back down into the chair. What was it with men pushing her back down into chairs all of a sudden anyway?

"Well I'm not laughing and take your hands off me!"

He moved back as if he'd been stung and continued moving until the width of the desk was between them. Turning, she watched as he unpinned the scrap of paper, his eyes lingering over her face as he continued to speak.

"The men, they spotted you first. Rexi recognised you from this," his fingers now tracing the line of her cheek. "And when he realised I'd fallen for you, he pinned this as a little memento." Folding the paper he took out his wallet and slipped it underneath the little plastic screen inside before replacing it in his back pocket.

"I know you don't believe me but it's the truth," his eyes finally meeting hers.

She sighed, now at a loss what to believe. She so wanted it to be true, but could she trust him? Hugging her arms around her she thought back to the last few days and the type of man he was. He'd promised not to do anything to hurt her and, apart from the picture now tucked away in his jeans, he hadn't; Rupert on the other hand…

"We were followed."

"Pardon?"

"We were followed over the weekend. There are photos; photos ready to be released to the press along with a story about how you're only after my money."

"Who would?"

"Rupert."

"I'm going to kill him," his eyes blazing.

"That's what he probably wants you to do. He's going to ruin you. You know that don't you? You attacking him would be the icing on the cake as well as ruining all this," her hands spreading around the room. "He'd love to see you locked up in gaol, too."

"What do you mean?" His gaze never leaving her face.

"Rupert is evil and he's won," leaning back in the chair. "He's the reason for your financial difficulties today. You have been having financial problems, I take it?" Her look suddenly soft.

"I've had a backer pull out if that's what you mean?"

"And tomorrow your other backer will too. I hope I was worth it!"

"Why would he do this…?"

"Because he wants me, or at least not me but the money that comes with me. I'm the cherry on top of his cake as far as he's concerned, although I'm not his usual type by all accounts. He's told me he's prepared to have a crack at me to see if he can loosen me up a bit," a rogue tear tracking down her cheek.

"*Mon Dieu*, what have I done?" He breached the distance between them in one stride and, cradling her within his arms stroked her hair off her face.

"You haven't done anything, Pascal. It is what it is. I'm sure Aunty Popsy didn't intend for men to be fighting over me like a dog with a bone but that's what it feels like." She raised her hand to his chin, relishing in the feel of rough stubble against her palm. "I've agreed to marry him."

"You've what!" He exploded, pulling away. "Over my dead body."

"Shush, stop talking like that, and anyway it's not up to you. It's the only way I can see for you to hold on to all this. This is so good, so noble. I can't let someone like Rupert spoil it."

"I won't let you do it."

"It's done, finished, finito, the end. The engagement will be announced in The Times on my birthday."

"When is…?"

"1st July, but this is the last time I can see you. I had to agree to his demands and then I made him contact your backers."

They were interrupted by the sudden ringing of the phone.

She could only hear his end of the conversation and rapid French really wasn't her thing, but she got the gist all the same.

"That was the backer who pulled out earlier apologising for the clerical error and that he was still on board." His white knuckles straining against his skin as he replaced the receiver. "If I had any guts, I'd have told him just where he could stick his money but the men need their wages."

"Of course they do. I just hope he doesn't sack anyone to prove a point. There have been enough sacrifices over this."

"Sarah I…" He knelt by her feet, his head now resting on her lap.

"It's all right," her hand stroking his hair like a child. It was her turn to offer comfort to this great, big, bear of a man who just like her had lost everything. "We'll get through this."

"But he'll…"

"He'll never get me. He'll never get what's deep inside; it's not mine to give anymore, Pascal."

"*Ma chérie.*" He leant back on his heels drawing her down on the floor beside him.

He was asleep now, a brown lock escaping onto his forehead, a sheen of moisture still lingering on his skin. Easing up off the floor she rubbed her hip, briefly smoothing the wrinkled flesh where skin had embraced concrete. At the time she hadn't noticed the hardness of the floor under the sleeping bag he'd spread out before lowering her on top. At the time she'd hadn't noticed anything except him; his mouth, his hands, his body. Everything was new and yet centuries old as inhibitions merged to unite both fantasies and dreams.

Pulling up discarded leggings she didn't feel either happy or sad. Yes this was goodbye, but it had to be if there was to be any sort of future for them outside of this madness. That's what she felt. She felt mad, reckless even as a blush scored her cheeks but for once she didn't care. She was mad with love for him, a love she knew deep down he returned with each and every heartbeat. She'd marry Rupert but she wouldn't live with him. In fact, she'd make it a term of the pre-nup that he'd insist on so he could gain full control of the eighty million. She'd have it set in stone that if he so much as touched her he'd lose it all. He made her sick with revulsion and loathing, but he wouldn't win in the end; he wouldn't win her.

Pulling her blouse over her head her eye snagged on the ring he'd placed on her finger hours before. Twisting it round she admired the way the ruby caught the light encased as it was with swirling gold tendrils weaved with six tiny seed pearls. He'd been carrying it around in his pocket long before he'd picked up the nerve to speak to her, she remembered with a tender smile. Now the ring would be a reminder, a reminder and a torment but she'd never remove it. She'd never remove it, her fingers lightly counting the pearls with the tip of her nail. Six pearls to remind her of the six most precious days that would have to last a lifetime.

Dragging on her cardigan, she thought about the immediate future only because she couldn't stay here. She couldn't stay in Paris with the sight of him just a window away to haunt her. She'd go back home. She'd have to because, apart from Cara's shoebox lounge, she had nowhere to go. She'd return home and look for some kind of teaching job and rent a little cottage far away from everyone. She'd be just like that girl in the photo but sadder. Then she'd had hope in her heart for a bright future, for a future full of potential and possibility. Now she was just a poor little poor girl with her sax for a friend. She wouldn't even be able to take Minou with her. It just wouldn't be fair to make him spend six months of his life in quarantine, not after what he'd been through and Cara wasn't allowed pets.

No, she'd ask just one thing more from this kind handsome man even now rolling on his side, his hand tucked up under his head in lieu of a pillow. Making up her mind was easy, leaving him now, leaving him forever was proving the hardest thing she'd ever been asked to do. As the sun finally started to appear over the rooftops, she knew these last few precious moments had come to an end.

She let her gaze wander across his face, his mouth, his throat one last time before pressed a silent kiss against his forehead and making her way out of the office.

Chapter Seven

14th May. My life is over. Welcome to my life.

Back in her apartment, the first thing she did was phone the airport to secure a seat on the next available flight. It didn't give her much time but that's exactly how she wanted it. Racing around the apartment like a mad woman she threw things into her bags with no thought for anything other than her grandmother"s gold watch ticking away the seconds on her wrist.

She managed to pack everything apart from Minou who was watching her from the back of the sofa with a blank-eyed stare. She finally persuaded him to clamber into the cardboard box she'd found by padding it out with her fluffiest towel just as the taxi hooted softly from the street below. All that was left was a quick call to Cara to come and pick up the keys before lugging all her worldly goods down four flights of stairs. With her heart now in residence across the road she closed the door on her life in France with a resounding slam.

"Hey *mademoiselle*, you can't bring that cat in here." The cabbie, just like cabbies across the globe frowned at the audacity of one of his customers bringing anything half unusual into the back of his cab.

Minou, a large handsome cat hiding his good looks under a scrawny exterior was unusual to say the least.

"Oh do hush, you'll scare him." She threw him a glowing smile, the one she practiced in the mirror before pestering Hopper's wife for another slice of her famed cherry and rhubarb pie. "Look, I'll give you a hefty tip if you can take me to the Avenue des Etats-Unis where I have every intention of leaving the cat." She added with emphasise. "Then you can take me on to the airport."

"How much?"

"Fifty euros."

"Done." He lifted the rest of her bags and, placing them in the boot turned back, one eye still on Minou. "Don't get me wrong *mademoiselle*; I love cats, just not in the back of my cab."

"Well, you won't have to worry about Minou for long will you *monsieur?*" She held the now meowing box even tighter on her lap. "You won't even know he's here."

"Harrumph."

Resting back against the seat, she forced her eyelids to close, reluctant to give in to any lurking temptations of turning her head towards the building, his building. She'd said her goodbyes earlier - that was all.

She didn't remember the flight. She didn't remember anything after she'd left a meowing Minou scratching at the window as he watched her climbing back into the taxi. She must have paid the taxi driver for getting her across town just in time. She must have stood at check-in behind, or in front of, a motley assortment of other passengers destined for Gatwick. She must have accepted, or more likely declined the drink offered but she couldn't remember. All she remembered was the look on his face when she'd told him about Rupert; Rupert and the future that lay ahead.

Arriving in Gatwick she made her way to the train station to catch the next train heading towards Sunnymeads, the nearest railway station to Cosgrave Manor.

It was only as the train approached the station she remembered no one would be waiting for her. Apart from Cara, no one knew she was heading home with her tail between her legs. With no taxi rank outside the small, rural unmanned station she had a very long walk ahead. Looking at the bashed up telephone box in disgust she couldn't even call anyone as the one thing she should have done when she'd returned to the apartment was put her phone on charge. In the race to catch the next flight it was the one thing she needed to remember and the one thing she'd forgotten.

Dragging her bags out of the train she looked around the deserted platform with a sigh, which soon turned into a scream at the sound of her name.

"Ah there you are, Miss Sarah."

The sense of relief at the sight of Hopper was just one thing too much. The tears that had refused to fall now streaked down her face in steady streams as if they'd never stop. The Hopper's were staff in her parents employ, something she was never allowed to forget. But to her this middle-aged couple were more than that. They were her friends. In truth all she wanted to do was throw herself into his arms and let him take over but years of training by her mother meant there was still that invisible divide to hammer down first.

"How did you know…?"

"Miss Cara phoned Beverley."

"So my parents?" She eyed him warily.

"Your parents are still away, Miss. They've popped down to St Tropez for a few days. They're not due to return until Monday week." He avoided looking at her, instead thrusting a sparkling white handkerchief into her hand with an embarrassed cough. "Come on, let's get you home."

He picked up both bags as if they were tissue paper light instead of being full of proverbial bricks, kitchen sinks and the odd statue or ten of the Eiffel Tower. "I hope you're hungry, Beverley has a feast prepared."

Was she hungry? She asked herself, following his stiff back out of the station and towards the waiting Bentley. She should be hungry. She'd missed breakfast, and last night's supper too as she remembered the champagne and other bits and pieces she'd offered to her neighbour. No, she wasn't hungry but she should be.

"Hop in the back, Miss, I'll have you home in no time."

"Can I sit in front, Hopper?" She'd wiped her face clean and now clutched the balled up hankie between tight fingers as if her life depended on it.

"Certainly Miss…"

"I do wish you'd call me Sarah," she added, examining the familiar grey-haired man pulling out onto the road.

She'd known Hopper all her life and had never seen him in anything other than the dark grey suit he habitually wore. Did he wear it on his days off? Did he sleep in it? If she rang the bell at 3 am would he appear fully dressed without a hair out of place, or did he have suitably conservative night attire instead? She just bet he wore one of those old-fashioned, striped night shirts with matching hat that came with its own built-in tassel.

Staring across at his profile, she realised she'd never questioned anything about the man who'd been resident at Cosgrave Manor for as long as she could remember. It was as if he was a stranger, a stranger she'd lived in close proximity to for most of her life. She thought he liked her, but did he really? After all, her father was the one paying for his service and his loyalty.

All of a sudden it interested her, he interested her. How did he spend his days off, for instance? Where did he disappear to for the last two weeks of July; the same two weeks every July? She wanted to get to know him, but would he want to get to know her, the real her? Would he even be bothered in making conversation outside the usual butler/employer speak? She was about to find out.

"Just Sarah? I couldn't do that, Miss. What would your parents say?"

"But you've known me forever, Hopper and I don't even know your first name?"

"It's Arnold, Miss."

"Now that figures." She threw him a twinkling smile.

"Why?"

"Well, let's just say, when it's just us, I'm going to call you Arnie, after Arnie Schwarzenegger, you know?"

He chuckled. "I do know. As long as it's not in front of your parents I'd be honoured er, Sarah."

"Thank you." Resting back in her seat she closed her eyes with a sigh. "Wake me up when we get there, Arnie."

But he didn't have to wake her. She knew instinctively when the car rumbled over the cattle ramps that she was nearly home. She loved Cosgrave Manor with a passion. She loved every stone and shrub, every blade of grass and every window and, looking up at the large, grey, stone, frontage there were many to love. She'd tried to count them once but had lost count at forty three: forty three bright shiny windows, and for the first time in her life she wondered who cleaned them. All those ladders to reach the top windows and not even one scaffolding rod to help.

"How many windows are there Arnie, I used to try and count them as a child but I always gave up?"

"Fifty five Miss, er Sarah, if you include the small circular one in the centre. Funny you asking that?"

"I wondered who had to clean them. Not you, you have enough to do."

"Bless you. No, not me. The Master and Mistress are very strict on what the butler can and can't do. Now the National Trust has taken over the management of the estate, they get a company in from London three times a year. The frames are original as you know so it's important not to get just anybody in."

"Of course it is," she said, staring up at the Georgian pile built in the Nineteenth Century by the first Lord Cosgrave, whose painting still presided over the dark oppressive hall. She'd tried to forget her parents signing over the upkeep and control of Cosgrave Manor even if it had made complete sense at the time. The day-to-day upkeep was astronomical and the roof caving in over the back bedrooms was the last straw in a catalogue of disasters that had drained her parents coffers beyond belief. Although as disasters went, it wasn't a patch on the one that had befallen Pascal, she reminded herself on a sigh.

So what if the next set of death duties would mean a forced sale? So what if her parents weren't able to entertain on the grand scale of old? At least they still had a roof over their head even if their part of the house was roped off and limited to three bedrooms instead of thirty three. They still had a fantastic lounge, and an amazing brand spanking new kitchen. They could still afford the services of Hopper and Mrs Hopper, not to mention the most amazing holidays imaginable.

Staring up at the frontage with its Neo-Classical Grecian pillars she could quite happily ignore the signs indicating where the hourly tours started. It was embrace the National Trust, their sympathetic maintenance and subtle renovations, or sell it to some rich Russian oligarch. She knew which option she preferred.

"Come along."

He frowned at the sight of her jumping out of the car instead of waiting for him to open the door.

"We can use the front entrance today without being mugged by some old biddy or other looking for the toilet," he flung over his shoulder as he headed for the boot. "We're so popular they've only allowed us one day off a week from those infuriating visitors trampling all over the place in their muddy size seven's."

"Don't let it worry you, Arnie." She clapped him on the back as she stared at the large mahogany front door. "It's what pays your and Bev's wages."

"I know, but it's not the same." He shook his head in despair.

"But it's the way of the world, Arnie. I do believe you're a snob," she added on a laugh. "I'd much rather be happy in a gatehouse than have to worry about how to heat this ruddy great pile of bricks."

As soon as the words were out, she realised the truth behind them. She'd be much happier in the gatehouse, Pascal's gatehouse, than anywhere else in the world. For all that she loved every stone and blade of grass of Cosgrave Manor; she loved Pascal a hundred, a million times more.

"But we don't have a gatehouse?" He gave her a sharp look before changing the subject. "Come along, Miss er Sarah. No need to look so glum. I'm sure Beverley will have the kettle boiled."

Entering the wide, marble-tiled hall pierced down the centre by a sweeping staircase her eyes widened at the sight of all the familiar paintings showcased against the striking green embossed wallpaper. This was still home despite all the changes and home was what she needed right now. Her fingers ran along the outline of the fireplace as she thought about what else she needed.

What she really needed was her mother. She wanted to be pulled into that tight Chanel filled embrace and tell her all about Pascal. For, despite everything, she was still her mother and still always there for her, except when she wasn't of course, suddenly remembering St Tropez with a grimace. The Hopper's would do for now, they'd more than do.

Walking into the sitting room was always a shock. Her mother had wreaked changes innumerable and now the former second sitting room was an oasis of cool blues instead of the pea green wallpaper it replaced. She'd stripped away the antique panelling once she'd discovered woodworm lurking. But instead of paying to have it sympathetically replaced, she'd called in an interior designer friend from London who would have ripped out everything including the priceless plasterwork ceiling, if the National Trust hadn't intervened with mutterings about British treasures being destroyed by some ignorant yuppie vandal from the city. So the plasterwork coving and ceiling rose remained, along with the cute little angel corbels that supported the original fireplace but that was all. Even the original floor had been covered with a thick white carpet to match the white leather sofas with coordinating sea blue cushions her mother had specially commissioned to match the wallpaper.

She followed Hopper across the room and along a short corridor before pushing the baize-covered door that led to the kitchen and on to the servant's quarters; in this case the small flat they'd created from the old scullery and boot room.

"Well well, if it isn't Miss Sarah. Aren't you a sight for sore eyes?" Beverley, sitting in front of the scrubbed pine table, pushed the bowl of half shelled peas away before starting to stand up.

"No, you just stay where you are." Sarah rushed forward to embrace her friend. "And you can drop the Miss, isn't that right, Arnie?" she added, throwing a sparkling look in his direction.

"Arnie is it? Well whatever next." But her eyes belied her words as she hugged Sarah even closer before standing up and turning towards the kettle. "What about a cuppa and then you can tell old Beverley all about it."

You're not old," she replied. Beverley hadn't changed a bit in all the years she'd known her. What with her chic bobbed hair, now a little grey around the edges and rosy cheeks: she was just the way she remembered when Hopper had brought her back to the house as his bride all those years ago. He'd said he'd found her under a rose bush, and to an impressionable five year old she'd believed him. Now she wondered how they'd actually met.

"I wish me ole back could hear you, child," she said, but with a smile on her face as she switched on the kettle and gathered together matching cups and saucers. Sarah wandered over to the American style fridge and, pulling it open removed a jug of milk.

"Here, you shouldn't be doing that…"

"Yes I should, I'm not completely helpless you know," she added, placing the jug on the table. "I see we're still getting milk fresh from the farm?"

"Too right, I can't be doing with that nasty bottled stuff from the supermarket. I send Hopper first thing in the morning with an empty jug to catch it as soon as it comes out of the pasteurizer." She set plates and forks beside the milk jug, pretty plates to match the cups and saucers. "If you're in a mind to help, I baked a cake after Miss Cara phoned. It's in the larder cupboard."

"Mmm, chocolate fudge." Their eyes met. "You really are a darling."

"Well, I thought you'd need a bit of feeding up."

"What, after three months in the gastronomic capital of the world?" She laughed.

"I can't be doing with all them fussy sauces and the like. Apart from the bread and cakes you can keep all that foreign muck."

"That's a little harsh, Beverley, although…" She paused, holding the fork between her lips; her lids closing over pleasure-filled eyes. "I have to admit I haven't tasted anything to rival your chocolate cake."

"There, you see…" Beverley pulled back her chair and, placing the earthenware pot on the little mat in the centre, proceeded to fill the Edwardian china cups with tea strong enough to strip varnish. "Something tells me you have news child, and it's not happy news?"

"No, but not now." She smiled. "Now I'm going to finish my tea and do the washing up while you sit there and drain the pot. If I don't wake up by supper time," she said, filling the gleaming white butler sink with water, "just leave me. I can always make myself a sandwich later."

Later, heading for the door, she paused, one hand on the frame her face suddenly serious. "If anyone calls I'm not expected back until tomorrow."

Chapter Eight

14th May. I never knew what having a broken heart meant until just now. My heart isn't broken, it's ruptured.

He woke with the soft golden sun shimmering on the wall over his head and he knew he was alone again, just as he'd always been alone. He'd always been a solitary figure running around on his uncle's estate with no one to play with apart from the servants and they were either too busy or less than interested in a scruffy orphan child.

He could vaguely remember his parents, distant shadowy figures that used to come in a cloud of perfume and cigar smoke to hug him goodnight. Sometimes in the small hours he squeezed his eyes tight and, with arms wrapped around him, tried to recall what it felt to be hugged like that. To be embraced by someone that loved him unconditionally for himself alone and not for what they could get out of him. But he could never get it right. He could never replicate or quite remember the feeling of security that was now only a vague faded memory.

There were of course plenty of women happy, more than happy to hug him as he made love to them. But that wasn't unconditional love, more unconditional no strings sex. There wasn't love involved, at least not on his part. And since he'd been trying to set up his business, there'd been no one. In truth he'd been too tired at the end of the evening to think of anything other than bed.

Draping the spare end of the sleeping bag across his chest he breathed in the remains of her scent as he tried to recapture the feeling of being held by the woman he loved. But already her fragrance was fading; soon all he'd have to remember her by was the cutting in his wallet and that was not going to be enough.

He'd loved her the first time he'd set eyes on her. He could even remember having to grab on to the rail in front of him as his gaze lingered on her body, her face, her scraped back hair. He'd felt punch drunk with the emotions exploding within his chest and only managed to drag his eyes away after Rexi had shouted at him for probably the millionth time to pass him another brick. And now with the sound of her voice and the feel of her hands fresh in his memory? What did he feel now except regret; regret and sadness for this the last hug, the last kiss, the last time.

She'd said she wouldn't see him again, and he knew her well enough to know she'd keep that promise even if it was only made out of some false sense of loyalty. She'd also said Rupert would break him. He didn't care about that. He'd only agreed because of the damage he'd do to Sarah along the way. She said he had dozens of photos which he'd showed her. Photos he'd happily flood both the French and UK press with and she'd end up with nothing. Her reputation would be in tatters and her parents would never speak to her again. Yes she'd inherit but a relationship; their relation could never survive with resentment at its heart. She'd grow to resent him and what his love had done to her. It was only this had made him agree to her request.

He sat up at the sound of the security railings being rattled, heralding yet another day. Bundling up the sleeping bag he was just in time to slip on his jeans and pull up the blinds before unlocking the door. There was nothing left for him now but work. He'd better just get on with it.

But he couldn't.

He couldn't get on with it because there was nothing to get on with. He was now a victim of his own hard work, a victim of his vision and finally a victim of his own success. The morning she'd disappeared out of his office and out of his life was when Le Figaro,

France's second largest newspaper published a double page spread on the birth of the *Le Monsieur Builder*. His project manager, arriving back on site, slapped the open newspaper on his desk almost upsetting the cold expresso and uneaten croissant Rexi had dropped on his desk hours earlier.

"Thanks for covering for me *patron*, but I think you'll have enough to be getting on with," his voice low as he tapped the article with his forefinger. "Now don't you be getting above yourself *Le Monsieur Builder*, not that the lads will let you. It's time for you to look for a new project and leave the building work to the experts."

"Perhaps, Pierre." His mind and his gaze turned towards the now empty apartment opposite. He suddenly had no enthusiasm for the building, just as he couldn't give a jot for the article staring back up at him.

He could hardly even remember the interview all those months ago when, keen to raise the profile of his work, he'd sent out letters of introduction to every newspaper across Paris. All he could remember was a meeting at *Le Bristol Hotel* with one of their up and coming journalists. He couldn't remember her name or indeed her face. He couldn't remember anything about that afternoon except her keenness to prolong the interview into the evening and beyond. Later he'd reasoned the absence of any article, after such a comprehensive grilling was more down to his polite refusal than any inherent dislike of what he was trying to achieve.

As part of him wondered at the journalist's change of heart, the other part was reliving over and over again waking up to find her gone. He'd raced across the street but he'd been too late. Madame Du Pont came out of her door chattering away about the champagne she was planning on having with her supper, but that's all she could tell him; that's all she knew.

She'd run away as he'd known she would and he didn't know where. She could have gone running to Rupert for all he knew, but he hoped not. Surely she couldn't after what had happened between them? She'd given herself to him; Rupert would be the last thing on her mind.

For the first time since he could remember, he left the site early. The Parisian sun was still bouncing off the new green shoots of the tall proud plane trees that lined the street when he pulled out of the car park and headed for home.

What a difference a day made, his mouth a grim line. It had taken one day, not even one day for investors to fly out of the woodwork keen to get a slice of what they now knew was the best thing to hit Paris since automatic baguette dispensers. The estate agents, so reluctant to list his apartments were nearly beating down his door in an effort to be part of the action. He would have laughed at the irony if his heart wasn't broken to the core. Now he had all the money in the world at his feet and yet he couldn't have the one thing that meant anything to him. He couldn't have her.

His men, so in tune with his ways, curtailed their congratulations, their faces wary as if they too felt his inner grief. It was only Rexi, the loudest of them all, who noticed the missing article from behind his desk. It was only him that put two and two together. It was only him that patted him on the shoulder and told him to go home.

Home, was it even that, his eyes travelling over the stone frontage he'd lovingly repointed brick by brick? It wasn't home; it was a house, an empty house. His mind stilled, his gaze snagging on a pair of beady eyes staring at him from the security of his bedroom window and suddenly the quiet car devoid of anything but his thoughts was filled with the echo of laughter.

* * *

She wandered aimlessly around her parents lounge, gently fingering her mother's collection of Lorna Bailey cats, her mind unable to fix on any way out of her current dilemma. With the house now full of strangers, she felt confined to the apartment; imprisoned as she watched from the window as they decanted from the stream of coaches, their greedy eyes roaming around for glimpses of the *landed gentry* they knew still resided here.

She hated them, all of them and now wished with all her heart her parents had accepted that offer from the Russian oligarch. At least then she wouldn't have to see their eager little faces, mouths agape as they gossiped and gloated about how the other half lived.

Turning back to the tea tray Beverley had dropped in only moments before she selected a wafer thin cucumber sandwich before sinking into the folds of the leather sofa. She wasn't hungry, but she knew she'd upset them both if she didn't make some kind of start on the three-tiered cake stand crowded with scones dripping with homemade strawberry jam and fresh cream from the farm not to mention the tiny melt in the mouth fairy cakes she used to love as a child.

She'd been home over two weeks; two weeks of waiting for the call that never came. She'd expected to hear from him by now. It didn't matter she'd told him not to contact her, those were only words; words he'd know she didn't mean. But instead of hearing from him, she'd heard from Rupert.

Her eyes flickered to her laptop still open on the email he'd sent from his work address. Trust him to fit her in between business meetings. He'd probably added her to his Outlook Calendar on a diary repeat come to think of it. He seemed to email her with remarkable regularity, and always at the same time, as she eyed his terse missive with a frown. If she was that important the very least she could do was ensure she was out when he eventually decided to pick up the phone.

What could she do? Her eyes now closed as she tried to think herself out of her predicament. What could she do? Was there anything she could do? She'd do anything not to have to marry him, but he held all the cards, marked cards ensuring that whichever way she turned he'd win. She couldn't even go to her parents because of the way he'd slime-balled his way into their affection.

Prising the wings away from the top of a fairy cake she licked away the butter-cream icing. Her mind tried to latch on to anything to make it all disappear, but there was nothing she could think of apart from murder; either hers or his, and that was all a bit drastic.

Popping the remainder of the cake in her mouth her eyes wandered across to one of the only antique pieces of furniture in the room; her grandmother's Kingwood ormolu writing-table. She didn't know much about it, only that her grandfather had bought it for her on their honeymoon as a belated wedding gift, their honeymoon in Paris.

It was a sign, it had to be. Jumping to her feet she longed now to follow the intricate floral marquetry with her fingers, the feel of the cool wood flooding her with so many happy memories that she felt tears spring from nowhere.

Her grandparents had loved each other with a passion her father often thought embarrassing but she didn't. She used to sit in the drawing room and listen as he tinkled away on the grand piano in the corner, his eyes never far from his wife sitting quietly as she worked on her tapestry. That's what she wanted, and that's what both Aunty Popsy and now Rupert had stolen from her. Slamming her hand down on the top of the desk was a mistake, the brittle cabriole legs creaking their distress.

"Sorry, it's not your fault," her fingers sliding an apology across its smooth surface, as a blush coursed through her cheeks at the idea of speaking to a table!

Surely to God this isn't what Aunty Popsy envisaged when she'd drawn up her will?

Her fingers flat on the table top suddenly clenched as the glimmer of an idea flickered across her field of vision, a glimmer of an idea she grabbed with both hands.

The will: maybe there was something in the will.

Her eyebrows pulled into a frown as she struggled to remember Rupert's words and something about a codicil. But what about a loophole; if there was a loophole she'd find a way of wriggling through it.

Funny that. Slinging her bag across her shoulder she picked up the heavy silver tray. Funny that Rupert seemed to know more about her affairs than she did.

"You shouldn't be doing that, Sarah," Beverley said out of nowhere, trying and failing to wrestle the tray off her. "And you've hardly touched your tea…"

"I wasn't really hungry." She smiled briefly as she began to stack her dishes beside the draining board. "Do you mind if I borrow your old mac?" her eyes now on the black gabardine hanging on a hook beside the door.

"I'm just going to pop into Wraysbury and I intend to pass myself off as the second scullery maid if anyone stops me."

"Second scullery maid is it," she said on a laugh. "You've been watching too much television, my love. I don't know what your mother will say, I'm sure. We use it when we're cleaning out the chicken coop. While you're there Hopper quite likes the smoked kippers from the fishmongers if you could pick up a couple?"

Chapter Nine

30th May. I'm not looking my best; I'm not smelling my best either, thinking about Hopper's kippers. I can't believe how the last few weeks in Paris have changed me; I wouldn't have dreamt of leaving the house looking like a tramp, now I don't care.

Pushing the door open of Messrs. Pike, Pidgeon & Prue was like jumping between the pages of a Charles Dickens novel. As far as she could make out, the décor, desk and even the receptionist were the exact same as the last time she'd visited many years earlier. All that was missing were gas lights and quills and she'd think she'd just walked through a time tunnel. The receptionist, rising to her feet even remembered her name.

"Good afternoon, Lady Sarah, how may I help you?"

"Hello," offering a shy smile. "I was wondering if Mr Pidgeon would be able to see me? I'm afraid I don't have an appointment, but I'm happy to wait."

"I'm sure that won't be a problem." She felt herself examined from head to foot and wished now she'd had the farsightedness to ditch the mud stained mac in the back of the Mini but it was too late now.

"May I take your, er, coat?"

A tide of colour rushed up her cheeks. "No, best not. Lord only knows what the brown stains are on the bottom. It's a disguise."

"A disguise?" The grey eyebrows arching over tortoiseshell frames.

"Mmm from the yokels. Downton Abbey has a lot to blame itself for and Wednesdays are our busiest day for sightseers; something to do with 20% off for the over sixties, or so I'm told."

"I see." Her eyes wide, as she smoothed pencil slim skirt over pencil slim knees. "I'll just find out if Mr Pidgeon is free."

Sarah took the brief respite as an opportunity to roll up Beverley's mac into a tight ball and stuff it under the sofa. Her parents would never forgive her if she saw old Mr Pidgeon smelling of what she suspected was either chicken poo or horse shit.

Standing up, she was just in time to pin a smile on her face and extend a hand to the elderly man making his way towards her with outstretched arms.

"My dear, so good to see you again and I do hear that congratu..."

"Mr Pidgeon," she interrupted only too aware of the tortoiseshell glasses now swivelled in her direction. "How good of you to see me at such short notice."

"Of course, of course. Come along to the office and let's see how I can help you." He turned bright blue eyes on his secretary. "Tea please, Maud, if you'd be so kind."

He only continued speaking when he'd taken up residence behind his desk; both elbows perched on faded green leather.

"I had that fiancé of yours popping in to see me yesterday…"

"Well, it's not official, so I'd appreciate it if you'd keep it private for the moment."

"Oh, of course, you can always trust your solicitor to keep things quiet," he said, chuckling at his little joke, only to become serious again at the knock on the door.

"Yes, on the desk is fine. Thank you, Maud."

Leaning forward, she spoke on a whisper because she was pretty certain she hadn't heard the sound of Maud's footsteps echo a retreat across the wooden floorboards. "Mr Pidgeon, I'd like to see a copy of my aunt's will."

"Certainly," his hand reaching out to press the intercom. "I'll just call Maud back to…"

"Don't you have a copy here? It would be a shame to disturb your secretary, she looked busy," her eyes roaming over the bulging shelves behind his desk.

"Actually, it probably doesn't look it, but we're quite modern at Pike, Pidgeon & Prue," he said, giving her a wink. "I can even work this old thing," tapping the side of the PC beside him. "And as wills are available online…" He booted up his machine and, after a couple of minutes, the sound of printing interrupted his cosy questions about how her parents were doing.

"Right then, it's all pretty straightforward." He glanced over the top of his half-moon specs. "Your aunt Portia, or Popsy as she liked to be known, in an effort to cut down on inheritance tax decided to leave everything to you when you reach the ripe old age of twenty-three instead of your father who, as her sibling, was her next of kin being as she died without issue. Got it?"

Her eyes widened at all the legal terminology but she did indeed get it!

"But that's not all, is it?"

"No, as you say, that's not all. It seems that she was well aware of how this would make you a target for fortune hunters so no, she didn't leave it to you outright. To meet the requirements of the will, you have to be in a serious public relationship by the time of your twenty-third birthday…"

"Hold on a moment," her eyes scanning the printout as she repeated his words back to him. "Serious public relationship, what does that mean? My father told me that if I wasn't engaged by then I'd forfeit everything to…?"

"The Battersea Dog's Home, yes that's quite correct, or at least the second part is." He paused and, removing his glasses, rubbed at his eyes for a moment. "Have your tea my dear and I'll try to explain. Your Aunt," he continued, his gaze now focussed anywhere and everywhere except at Sarah. "Your aunt was an amazing woman, but you probably don't remember her?" His eyes flicking back briefly.

"I was only twelve when she died. I knew she was a very talented sculptress," she answered, placing the bone china cup back against its saucer with a steady hand. "I remember she used to blow in and out with that friend of hers, arms full to the brim with presents but that's about all. Father said she was too tied up in her glamorous life in New York to moult away in a mausoleum like Cosgrave Manor."

"That's true, but only up to a point. She couldn't stay in England living the way she wanted, so she decided on New York where she could melt into the background."

She blinked as she worked out what he was trying to tell her, everything finally falling into place. The reason the will had been worded in such a way. The way her mother would be carefully polite but no more. The awkwardness of her father. The friend, Margot something or other, who was always there in the background.

"So what you're trying to tell me, but not in so many words, is that if I was in a serious relationship with, let's say for arguments sake, another woman, I'd still be able to inherit?"

"Er, exactly."

Was that a slight reddening of his cheeks she saw? Surely not. She kept her smile to herself. Well, well, well and her parents had never so much as dropped a hint, but then again they wouldn't. In those days it would have caused such a scandal.

"But that's not going to affect you now is it?" His eyes finally meeting hers again. "Not now you're engaged to Rupert. Your parents will be delighted considering he owns the land bordering theirs."

"Mr Pidgeon, we're not formally engaged as I said and my life isn't some Jane Austen parody," she added, trying to stem the sudden surge of anger that threatened to overtake what was in effect, a mellow conversation. "The fact Rupert bought that derelict castle is of little interest as I'll never be living there."

"But surely if you're married?"

"There's a big *IF* in that question." She stared at him across the desk, He was a kind man, she could see that. A kind and honourable man who could have no idea what the likes of Rupert would engineer to lay his hands on her inheritance. If she continued in this vein, she'd only upset him. Picking up her bag and clutching it to her lap she stood up from the chair. "So just to reiterate, I need to be engaged before or on my twenty-third birthday, and if I am...?"

"And if you are, you'll inherit quite a sizeable amount, in cash. There are some shares and properties included, like her New York apartment and a cottage somewhere in Martha's Vineyard too, although..."

"Although?" she questioned softly, her eyes pinned to the unaccustomed stillness in the face opposite.

"Although the Martha's Vineyard cottage does have a condition attached." He pulled out a handkerchief, unfolding it before blowing his nose. "Your aunt's friend has a life enjoyment," his eyes finally meeting hers.

"Oh, is that all?" She laughed. "I thought you were going to tell me it was haunted or the scene of a murder or something. They both sound delightful. And my er... and Rupert knows all this?" Her eyes focussing again as he arched his hands in front of him. She'd been hoping for so much from this meeting. Some wriggle out clause that would mean marrying Rupert wasn't the only option open to her but there was nothing apart from the knowledge that Mr Pidgeon was on her side. That would have to do for now.

"Mr Reynolds–Smythe, of course, knows the contents of the will as it is public knowledge but that's all." He paused and met her gaze with a serious expression stamped across his features. "He was keen to know how much you'd be worth, all the nitty gritty valuations and bank accounts now you're an item, shall we say. I had to ring for my secretary to help me get rid of him in the end; no one gets past Miss Short."

"That I can well believe."

As soon as Sarah had left the office, he buzzed for Maud.

"If Mr Reynolds-Smythe calls again, tell him I'm not available, would you? It's a clear conflict of interest as I'm not representing him."

"I hear congratulations are in order…?"

"Well, you hear wrong, Maud." He peered at his secretary over the top of his glasses. "I've known that girl since she was a baby and if she ends up marrying him, I'll eat my hat." His gaze now on his old fashioned trilby perched on top of the coat-stand.

"Yes, Mr Pidgeon; lovely girl, apart from her strange taste in clothes."

"What are you babbling on about clothes for, I hadn't noticed! Now back to work with you or we'll never get home."

"Ah there you are, Lady Sarah. Mr Reynolds–Smythe phoned. He'd like to take you out for supper and a show this evening." Her lips pursed.

So she was back to being Lady Sarah now was she? Her eyes followed Beverley's movements as she pummelled dough as if she was in the boxing ring.

She knew she was upset. She had no idea what Rupert had told her but presumably it was enough to distress her. Walking over she gave her a quick hug even as she whispered in her ear.

"Bev, don't believe everything you hear."

"He called you his fiancée." She gave up on the dough, throwing it in the prepared loaf tin before slamming it in the oven. "If that rises I'll be a Dutch uncle."

"I'm sure it'll be lovely." And if it wasn't, she'd eat it all the same.

Sarah turned towards the kettle and, flicking the switch, spooned out Nescafe into a couple of the earthenware mugs her parents so despised. "Where's Arnie, will I make him a mug?"

"He can sort himself out."

"You haven't had a row have you?" she said, throwing her a suspicious glance as she poured hot water into the mugs.

"No luv, me and Hopper never row, just the occasional misunderstanding."

"And?"

"And," her face turned away. "And he says I was to mind me own business about you and…"

"I wouldn't want to be the cause of an argument between you two."

"You'd never be that, my luv." She threw her a smile. "Hopper and me are just fine…"

"I never did find out which rose bush you met under?"

"Rose bush is it? Is that what he told you?"

"Well, as I remember, he went away for his usual two week holiday and came back married?"

"That he did." Her eyes misty. "It was one of them romances that are only meant to happen in books. Our eyes met across the dance floor and…"

"Oh, you met in a club then?"

"Not quite a club, a dance studio: the Rose Bush dance studio in Blackpool. We go back there every year even though we're a bit past it now. We were both practicing for the IBDC. My partner…well, let's just say my partner had a roving eye, not to mention a roving hand so I dumped him."

This conversation was going from surreal to just downright confusing. She'd never in a million years have put Hopper as a dancer and as for Beverley, as much as she loved her, she couldn't imagine her wearing one of those glamorous Strictly costumes.

"What on earth is the IBDC, apart from sounding like some horrible disease?"

"The International Ballroom Dancing Competition at the Royal Albert Hall. We won with our tango that year, our greatest triumph considering we'd only just met," she continued. "I have some photo's somewhere if you're interested, as well as an old costume or two?"

"I'd love that, Beverley." Reaching out she took her hands within hers. "You know, as a child, I often wished you and Arnie were my parents instead of…"

"Ah, you shouldn't say that, child. Your parents mean well as you know. They're just a bit too…"

"Full of their own importance?"

"You could say that, but they're good people. They've been good to us. Nothing's ever too much trouble and the little flat they created when the National Trust moved in - money was no object."

"I know. It's just you were always there for me when my parents were off gallivanting. If it wasn't for Arnie doing the school run and you mothering me with cake and kisses I'm not sure where I'd have ended up. Certainly not in France or indeed the Sorbonne, so in a way what's happened is all your fault…" She paused, hesitant now if she should confide any further or wait until her parents return. But before she could make up her mind Hopper burst through the door with a basket full of fresh eggs in one hand and a clothes brush in the other.

"Bloody Nora! The mac you use for the chickens. I've just remembered where I've left it," she said with barely contained laughter. "Oh well, they'll probably find it eventually."

"That reminds me, did you remember those kippers for Hopper's tea?"

"Mmm. They're in the same place as the mac!"

Walking over to her father's drinks table, she lifted up the cut-glass Waterford crystal decanter before pouring herself a thick measure.

"If you want one, help yourself," she said, perching on the arm of the sofa, one slim ankle all there was to see under her floor length black dress.

Rupert had called for her a little after six, not taking no for an answer. He'd found her still in her jeans lying in the middle of the floor with a book.

"Really Sarah, aren't you ready yet? If you don't get a move on they may not even let us in. You know how sniffy the Opera House is at interrupting performances for latecomers."

Well that's no loss, she thought, slowly getting to her feet. Having to sit beside Rupert for more than five minutes as he talked his way through Madame Butterfly, her favourite of all Puccini's operas was more than she could bear.

She'd first heard the music snuggled up beside her grandmother while her grandfather ran over the notes from memory, music so special she couldn't abide to have it spoilt by the store of smarmy comments Rupert was famed for.

"I'm ready," she said, placing the priceless David Wolff goblet on the table with care.

"One of these days you're going to break that and then where will you be; ten grand poorer!"

"But with very happy memories of my grandparents who insisted that it was to be used…"

"When we're married that will be residing in the bank along with those diamonds," his eyes focussing on the star brooch and matching earrings. "I'll get you paste ones to wear instead."

"What, along with a paste engagement ring?" Her voice challenging.

"Patience, princess," he murmured, lowering his head to her ear before aiming a sudden kiss against her lips, only to get her cheek as she turned just in time. "You'll get your ring. Come along now or we really will miss that first act and I hear the Royal Box will be in use tonight."

He left the rest unsaid, but she was easily able to fill in the gaps. The only reason he'd chosen tonight was presumably because he'd been given a tip off. He was still determined to crawl his way to the top of the ladder, and her title in addition to her fortune added more than a few rungs.

Arriving at Covent Garden, the sight of all those My Fair Lady pillars always had her heart leaping about in her throat, despite the fact her grandparents and then her parents had been bringing her here ever since she could remember. At first for the matinee and then, when she was twelve, for her first taste of an evening performance followed by late supper, always at Café Murano. When she was a student she'd attended with friends and even once or twice by herself, but never in a box.

Rupert followed her up the narrow stairs, through the little curtained-off door and into a private room, private except for Rupert huffing and puffing behind her. But she ignored him, her hand already reaching out to feel the plush, red velvet curtains running through her fingers before taking her seat on one of the matching velvet covered chairs. She heard him dragging his chair nearer, stage whispering into the side of her neck.

"Don't look now but the Royal Box is full."

"Okay."

"Okay what?"

"Okay, I won't look now," she added before turning away, her eyes trained on the stage as the curtain lifted.

In turning away, she forgot where she was or indeed who she was with as Puccini's poignant story of unrequited love poured over and across her, capturing her within the folds of the story. With each successive note, with each successive word, she wasn't Sarah Cosgrave with her cocked up love life and impending marriage that was doomed from the moment he'd coerced her into accepting his hand. No, she was the hauntingly beautiful Cio

Cio San awaiting the return of her lover and the father of her child, her heart breaking with every empty tide.

The music swelled to embrace her soul as tears started their weary journey across her cheeks. An echo of something had invaded her consciousness; a crossover of something almost tangible that had been peering up from the depths of her subconscious for days now only to be pushed back down with an indifferent hand. But now the horror of her discovery made her catch her breath in alarm as she tried to count back just when she'd last had her period, certainly not since returning to England.

Unlike Cara who could mark it down on a calendar and plan her life accordingly she had never been the most regular or indeed the most interested: there was little point. She didn't have a lover to prepare herself for, and if she had she'd go on the pill. It's not as if she was stupid or anything. But with Pascal it hadn't mattered, and it should have. By God it should have mattered, her eyes filling again with tears. Blinking them away she struggled to remember just when her last cycle had been. She still had that pack of Tampax in the bottom of her wash bag and she'd bought that from the supermarket next to her old apartment six weeks ago or more.

"For goodness sake clean yourself up a bit," Rupert interrupted her thoughts, stuffing a tissue into her hand. "You've managed to smear mascara everywhere. I really don't see what you're crying at. You must have seen it a million times."

She scrubbed under her eyes before gathering her evening bag and wrap, unable to do more than follow him back down the stairs and out into the waiting car. She had too much to think about and, having to pause every couple of seconds beside Rupert as he schmoosed his way out of the building, was tantamount to torture by a thousand stares. Of course he had to introduce Lady Sarah, his fiancée, to anyone and everyone that caught his eye. Why else had he brought her? She wondered what he'd say if she introduced herself as his pregnant fiancée; his pregnant with another man's child fiancée. She wondered what he'd say then. She wondered what he'd do. Would he still want to marry her? Of course he would. She was his new cash point.

Finally, sinking her head back against the seat, she allowed her hands to rest nonchalantly across her lap, her thumbs gently massaging the slight mound of her belly.

She had some choices. Women in her predicament always had choices, but they weren't choices she was going to make. The only choice for her was to have the baby they'd made. She'd bring it up in a cherished happy home but that's as far as her dream would take her at the moment. She really should think about passing it off as Rupert's, her eyes peering at his smug self-satisfied face. That would mean she'd have to sleep with him soon, probably even tonight and her gag reflex just wasn't that strong. Perhaps if she puked up all over him he might change his mind about the wedding, something worth considering.

She heard him tap on the window that separated them from the liveried driver. "To the Savoy and snap on it, I've champagne on ice."

Oh God, that's all she needed, but one look at his set face and she knew she wouldn't win and was it worth it anyway? At least she'd be in a public place so the opportunity for him to maul her would be minimal if the waiters at the Savoy were the same as the ones at the Ritz. She'd known he'd try it on, but one word in his ear about them being in direct sight of the now heaving Royal Box and he'd jerked his hand back on to his lap where it had remained for the length of the performance.

Working on autopilot she allowed him to escort her to a central table before agreeing to his suggestion of caviar followed by lobster, even as she wondered why the only food men seemed to want to serve her were foul tasting fish eggs and what amounted to overgrown prawns. Her fingers lifted to her lips as she remembered the one man who'd dared to be different; the one man, the only man brave enough to serve her buffalo wings. She liked buffalo wings.

"You're very quiet. Cat got your tongue?" he said, laughing at his joke. "Although I must say, I do like the new acquiescent Lady Sarah. What about staying over tonight, hmm." His eyes peering into hers. "We can have a trial run before the honeymoon."

"And what if my parents arrive and find me absent, or even worse, I could fall pregnant?" Her voice quiet, her mind a quandary of thoughts.

Would it be such a bad thing? She should just do it with him. That would be the easy option and the one she was sure many women had chosen in the past. Although he'd said he didn't want any more children, he wouldn't be a bad father, just an absent one which suited her down to the ground. But with bile pooling in the back of her mouth she knew she couldn't, she'd grab a sword just like Cio Cio San. Although a kitchen knife might be easier to obtain in this day and age. Hysterical laughter, just like the bile before it, had to be swallowed back down her throat. No, she wouldn't do anything drastic, but she'd have to do something and pretty quick if her maths was correct. Just how long would it be before she started to show? There was so much she didn't know and no one to ask.

"That's not going to happen anytime soon." His fat fingers running themselves up and down her arm, pummelling her flesh like a trainee masseuse destined to fail their finals.

"Why's it not going to happen, it's not like I'm on the pill or anything?"

"As if I'd trust you to remember to take it," his eyes narrowing, his fingers starting to hurt. "How do you think I ended up with four kids; by trusting my beautiful, scheming wife that's how. As soon as she'd popped out that last brat she shacked up with her hairdresser and took me to the cleaners." Dropping her arm back against the table with a clatter he picked up his glass and drained it before slopping in more so it slipped over the sides. "No, I won't be having more kids. If I do I'll be suing my urologist." He looked up at her across the top of his glass. "Don't look so worried my dear. You'll be safe with me and I'll treat you like a princess as long as..."

"As long as I do what you say, is that it? Sounds very much like a prison doesn't it?"

"Would a gaoler provide you with this, hmm?" He took a box out of his pocket and, flicking open the top, revealed a huge solitaire diamond nestling against the blue velvet interior. Grabbing her hand before she had the foresight to hide it on her lap, he clumsily slid it in place.

"There, you're mine now." He threw her a salacious smile as he dragged her hand to his lips just in time for the first of many camera flashes to explode in her face.

"You had it all planned didn't you," the words ripping across the table without a care for who was listening. "The ring. The opera to soften me up. The best table in the Savoy and then what; calling in a few favours from some media friends? So, which newspaper am I going to grace the front cover of tomorrow then?"

Her pupils finally adjusted to see the swell of photographers envelop the table like rats even as the head waiter started shooing them out of the restaurant with a well-manicured hand.

"All of them, my dear. Now let's get back to enjoying our meal shall we? The Savoy isn't the place for histrionics now is it?" he added, pouring out a large glass of champagne and pushing it in her direction. "I've arranged an appointment with your solicitor for tomorrow, just so we can get a pre-nup organised."

"Well, cancel it." She shoved the champagne away, instead picking up the glass of sparkling water the waiter had kindly provided.

"I think not."

"I saw Mr Pidgeon today, as a matter of fact." She saw him glance at her sharply. "That's surprised you, hasn't it? Yes, I decided to reacquaint myself with Aunt Popsy's will." She watched him relax slightly.

"Oh, there's no need to worry your pretty, little head about such financial matters, darling."

"Oh, darling, but I think there is, after all Aunt Popsy was only trying to protect me from fortune hunters," she said, tucking a stray curl back in place. "Why so quiet Rupert, cat got your tongue?"

"Now listen here," he replied, trying and failing not to raise his voice, much to the interest of the couple sitting at the next table.

"No, it's your turn to do the listening. I said I'd marry you. You didn't really give me any choice but, as per the wording of the will, I don't get my inheritance until I've had my birthday. You, my dear husband-to-be are not legally entitled to a penny until after the wedding," her voice almost a whisper as she smiled sweetly at the buxom battle-axe next door. If she leant any closer she'd offer her a seat. "After this evening, I don't want to have anything to do with you until my birthday party, which I suppose I'll have to invite you to. If you so much as ask about me, the deal is off."

Back once more in the car, all was silent, too silent. Rupert was a sharp cookie, he wouldn't have been able to crawl himself out of the gutter if he wasn't. He'd worked his way up that proverbial ladder and now intended to use both her name and her fortune to reach the top rung, something beyond the wildest dreams of a lowly butcher's son from Coventry. She felt his gaze on her chest, her legs, her lips as she tugged her wrap further across her shoulders, her eyes snagging those of the fatherly man driving them home.

"You think you're so clever don't you? Not so clever considering you're all alone. I think I'll just take a down payment…" His hand moving to his belt.

She leant forward and knocked on the little glass partition separating them from the driver before he could stop her, her face deathly pale.

"There's a Tesco's Express up ahead if you wouldn't mind stopping for a minute please."

"Right you are, Miss," he replied, turning left at the next roundabout before pulling up outside.

"If this is some kind of trick?" He looked her in the eye before smiling, his hand now reaching for the door handle. "It's all right, my dear. I'll go. Can't have you traipsing around Tesco's like that. What do you need, sweets, chocolate, flowers?"

"A box of Tampax, regular." She lifted her purse, rooting around for the twenty she'd slipped in the side pocket in case of emergencies.

"Oh, for God's sake!" he exploded, catching the smarmy expression on the driver's face before slamming his door shut.

"If you think I'm going to... Just get out, but if you're not back in five minutes, I'll send him looking for you," his hand waving in the direction of the man up front.

The next morning came around far too quickly. Of course she hadn't been able to sleep a wink after he'd dropped her outside like a bag of dirty washing. If it hadn't been for the sympathetic arm of the chauffeur helping her up the steps, she wasn't sure if she'd have made it.

She would have laughed at the supercilious look on Rupert's rude brattish face, but she was in no mood for laughter. If something didn't happen pretty soon she'd be married to him. She'd already managed, through no fault of her own to be conned into a public announcement of her troth. There was no way he was going to let her get away now all that lolly was staring him in the face. Come July she'd be an heiress, and he'd be desperate to slide a wedding ring beside the ice cube currently weighing her finger down.

The first thing she did on reaching the sanctuary of her room was remove the ring and place it in the bottom of her jewellery box, her eyes lingering on the ruby she'd had to move to her other hand. She'd promised never to remove it and, whatever happened, it was a promise she intended to keep.

Grabbing the pregnancy kit from her bag, she stared at the instructions before heading into the bathroom. She didn't need any blue line to confirm what she already knew in her heart. They should have used a condom. But it was too late now, far too late, her eyes focussing through an outline of tears at the two horizontal lines filling the little round window.

She was twenty-two and up the duff with another man's child. It could be worse but at the minute she couldn't quite see how.

She must have fallen asleep as dawn eased its amber glow over the horizon because the next thing she knew there was a soft knock on the door as Beverley came in with a cuppa.

"I wouldn't have woken you, but it's almost ten o'clock and Miss Cara has been on the phone since seven," she said, arranging the cup and saucer just so on the bedside table before continuing. "You're to check your emails, but I've a nice bit of breakfast ready."

"I'm not really hungry."

"What, I can't tempt you with even a little toast and some of me homemade marmalade?" she wheedled.

"Well, just a couple of slices." She smiled before reaching across the bed to where she'd thrown her iPad last night.

Minimising all the pages on pregnancy, she clicked open her email account and was hit in the face by photo after photo of Pascal.

Cara's email didn't say much, but it didn't have to. The images spoke only the truth. She wouldn't have believed her words, but photos? The glossy full sized images of him in various poses by his building and then less formal ones of him snapped on the arm of a string of different dolly birds. Paris had finally taken Pascal de Sauvarin to their hearts and was parading him across all the tabloids and TV stations like a lump of prize meat. Up until that moment she'd had some thought of whisking herself back to France. He had a right to know about the baby, his baby but now... now she didn't know what to do.

The phone piercing through her thoughts was a welcome interruption.

"At last, where have you been?"

"And good morning to you too, Cara," her voice holding a laugh. "The Hopper's must have diverted my line; I didn't get in till quite late. So what's up in lovely Paris?" Her eyes roaming across Pascal's face, a face she knew better than her own.

"Oh, same old. You got the articles I sent you? That Pascal of yours has caused a media frenzy over here, let me tell you. He's well on his way to making his first million. There's even talk of him meeting with the President..."

"Oh really," her eyes filling with tears as they lingered on his face. He didn't need her now. He didn't need her money, and he certainly didn't need to be stranded with a baby. She'd lost him. Had she ever had him? The echo of a smile shimmered and then faded. He was hers but only for one night. Now he belonged to France, and she belonged to Rupert.

"I always knew he'd make it. I'm very happy for him," she said, switching off the iPad and flinging it across the bed. "I hope you'll be able to come to my birthday party, not that I've arranged much but there's bound to be cake."

"Sweetie, I wouldn't miss it for the world." There was a pause. "You are sure you're doing the right thing marrying Rupert? The last time we spoke you called him a toad."

"Cara, I don't love him or anything but it's for the best really…"

"But I thought you and your builder had something special; you know, like me and Aaron…?"

"No, that was only sex," her heart ripping in two as soon as the lie left her lips. As much as she loved her friend, she couldn't let her interfere in her life.

Saying goodbye, she placed her cup back on its saucer with a little chink, before letting her head flop back against the pillow, any thoughts of a romantic reunion shattering around her. Her eyes closed on the world, a world she'd suddenly grown to hate, loath, despise even, or was it just the people that inhabited it; people apart from the likes of Cara and the Hoppers, and her parents.

Her parents weren't too bad, just misguided as to what was best for their only child. If she'd been a boy or even a horse, they'd have been different but she wasn't. She didn't fit any mould they'd been used to and therefore they'd left her to her own devices to be more or less brought up by the servants. With a sigh of regret she curled up on her side, her arms cradling her belly and let the tears take over.

Chapter Ten

1ˢᵗ June. I'm brave, brave or stupid to be running after a girl that's now engaged to someone else; probably both! I know she doesn't love him, but will my love be enough? We've had such a short time together, seconds; seconds to last a lifetime.

Despite Sarah telling him what to expect, he felt totally unprepared for his first sighting of Cosgrave Manor. In his mind's eye, he'd thought it to be an English version of Chateau Sauvarin but any similarity to his humble abode ended at the enormous wrought-iron gates. The drive was almost a mile long and obviously maintained to a high standard. It didn't matter that it was now run as a National Heritage site, all that mattered as he stared up at the massive grey frontage was just how much she was out of his league. His family home, despite the turret follies was piddling in comparison. No, there was no comparison.

Slinging his rucksack across one shoulder he waited for the remains of the coach party to exit before dawdling along at the back. He must be the youngest taking the tour, the youngest by about forty years but it was the only way he could think of getting to see her. It would have been so much easier to have hired a car at the airport but then what? He couldn't just turn up unannounced for afternoon tea, not after what had happened. She'd told him not to visit, his face grim as he remembered those weren't exactly her words. But never seeing her again just wasn't an option, at least not for him. He had no idea what he'd find, but he had a pretty good idea, his eyes falling again on one of the many newspapers scattered across the coach's blue flock seats.

Game, Sax and Match for Lady Sarah seemed to sum it up nicely. She'd announced her engagement to that dunderhead only this morning. So the reason for his visit didn't even exist anymore unless he could persuade her to marry him instead, and that wasn't likely to happen any time soon.

Stepping on the smooth weed free path, he stooped to pick up a cardigan before handing it to the grey-haired woman ahead who'd just dropped it. He couldn't compete with all this, but that wasn't going to stop him from trying.

The last couple of weeks had proved to him that building state of the art apartments wasn't all it was cracked up to be. He had no desire to spend even one more second than he had to away from her and that included attending all the interviews that seemed to descend out of nowhere. In desperation, he'd promoted Rexi to media director and escaped back to the gatehouse to pack a bag and drop Minou off at the local cattery before catching the next plane to London.

Politely refusing an invitation to accompany the group of three elderly ladies ahead on the tour he tried to slip away, only to be stopped by an over-zealous hand on his sleeve.

"No, not that way sir; the visit starts over here by the stables."

He allowed himself to be led back to the queue only to retrace his steps as soon as the tour guide's back was turned. He wasn't interested in the stables, or indeed horses at the moment and he could do without hearing just how far an orphaned architect was out of their league, and a French one at that. It would take him a long time to forget that jibe of Rupert's about where he'd parked his baguette.

Entering the hall he threw a quick look at the old whiskered gentleman staring down at him and he felt the first strand of sympathy for her. His eyes snagged on the rancid green wallpaper interspersed with similar paintings of what must be long dead relatives. It was worse than living in a mausoleum and he hadn't even started on the moth eaten stag's head nailed above what looked to be an authentic marble fireplace. He could see why she'd escaped; first to university and then to the Sorbonne. He wondered how she'd borne it for so long. From what he'd seen of her parents they would have been absent at best. At least he'd had loving parents and then his uncle to watch out for him, but she'd had no one.

Throwing a swift look across his shoulder, he unhooked the red rope and headed towards the door ahead marked private.

"Can I help you, Sir?"

The formal tone stopped him his tracks. Turning, he found himself staring into the questioning gaze of what looked to be a business man decked out in a tailored grey suit and matching plain grey tie, both in stark relief to the starchiness of both his shirt and his tone.

"I came to see Lady Sarah."

"She didn't inform me she was expecting guests," their eyes locking.

"Er, no. She's not expecting me. It's a ..."

"Surprise?" he added, the slight softening of his tone turning it from Antarctic to only Artic.

"Yes, that's right," he said, allowing his breath to seep through his teeth.

God, this was worse than the Spanish Inquisition, and just who was this man; her guard, another suitor?

He noted the sudden twinkling eyes and something clicked in his memory-bank about a butler, a butler with a rather unusual name or he'd have had no chance of remembering.

"If you could tell her Pascal de Sauvarin is here to see her, Mr Hopper is it?"

The smile broadened at the use of his name. "If you could follow me sir, I'll see if Lady Sarah is available, and it's just Hopper. I take it you met her in…?"

"Paris, yes."

"Exactly, sir." Pushing open the door to the drawing room he gestured him ahead before pulling on an old fashioned tapestry rope by the fireplace.

He watched the door open to reveal a tall slim woman dressed in a simple grey shift dress with matching pumps and kindly blue eyes.

"Beverley, Monsieur de Sauvarin would like some tea while he awaits Lady Sarah."

"Well he's in for a long wait, she's still asleep," her eyes taking their time to meander across his face. "You just settle yourself there while I give her a shake, there's a pile of papers on the table."

"I've read them!"

"I'm sure you have." She smiled at him, a little more than kindness in her expression, "I'll make you a bit of toast too. She hates eating alone."

She looked tired.

That was his first thought. She looked tired and worried, or should that be wary, or both? His hand scrubbed across his chin as he took in her towel dried hair left to run loose down her back, almost to her waist. How he wanted to run his hands through her hair and across her face and shoulders, smoothing all that tension. That was his second thought and one he quickly squashed as he watched her cross the room to kiss him on both cheeks.

Her lips, barely touching his skin, left a mark all the same, a mark akin to burning, but he left his hands by his side. His touch wouldn't be welcome. This was a very different Sarah to the one he'd cradled against his breast as she'd slept beside him. This was a stranger.

"Come and join me," her voice hostess soft, her hand indicating the laden plates Beverley and Hopper were arranging on the intimate table in the corner. "It will only upset them if we don't at least try everything," she added, taking a triangle of toast from the rack and smearing it with butter.

He laughed, but it wasn't a happy sound. "This, this is so English, Sarah." His hands spread wide. "I never imagined you living like this with servants answering your every whim."

"The Hoppers are not servants," she interjected, placing her untouched toast back on her plate and meeting his eyes for the first time. "They're my friends."

He ignored her interruption. "Here was I thinking you'd be all alone, that you'd even be pleased to see me a little and you're just some posh girl being fussed over like a spoilt…"

"Shut up!" Pushing herself back from the table and heading for the fireplace, her arms folded across her chest. "What right have you to speak to me like that? If you've come here to insult me, I'll ring my *servant* to escort you off the premises."

"I thought I had every right, but obviously not."

Raking his hands through his hair he realised what a mess he was making of everything. It wasn't meant to be like this. She was meant to run into his arms while she told him how much she adored him, wasn't she? But looking at the obstinate set of her chin, the glare of her gaze, the stiffness of her back, there was more likelihood of her standing on the table and dancing the Can Can than there was of her smiling at him. He eyed her warily, his mind struggling to think of something to say to make it all better. He was out of words. He was out of thoughts. He was out of ideas. For inspiration, he shifted his eyes around the room only to rest them on the pile of newspapers waiting in a neat folded pile on the sofa-table.

He was still hurting from arriving in London only to be confronted by the headlines screaming out from every tabloid and broad sheet and then, to cap it all, he'd spent the last two hours cooped up beside a couple of fervent royalists salivating over every word. Looking at her he could still hear their voices throbbing around his head.

"He's a bit older than her, don't you think?"
"Maybe she likes them experienced."
"Mmm maybe she won't even be able to wear white."
"Maybe she had to get married?"
"I wonder how much he paid for the ring. He doesn't look the type to buy a fifty quid fake from down the market." Their pupils dilated as they devoured the photos with all the finesse of hungry wolves gulping their prey.

His eyes flickered to her stomach in alarm as he remembered all too well what had haunted him ever since that morning. He'd always been so careful, but *careful* hadn't crossed his mind that night; any ideas of *careful* had been suppressed by other more important feelings, at least more important at the time. To allow lust and passion overtake everything was such a stupid elementary mistake; a mistake he hoped to God they weren't going to have to pay for. An unwanted child. His thoughts stuttered to a halt for, in truth no child of theirs would ever be unwanted; inconvenient maybe, but not unwanted.

Other thoughts crowded in then only to be ruthlessly quashed. He wouldn't allow himself to think about her fears over having a child; he couldn't. He had enough problems without adding illness, her illness to their current difficulties.

His eyes moved to her hand, her left hand, his heart clenching. She'd said she'd never remove his ring. He frowned at the empty finger, his mind picturing Rupert's statement diamond as he tried to figure it out. Perhaps he'd got it wrong, and they wore their ring on the right hand, his eyes shifting to catch the glimmer of red just visible under her clenched fist. It was the first thing in the last five minutes that allowed him to hope just a little, but it would take a lot more than a glimpse of gold to rectify the situation.

"You're not wearing your diamond." He'd have to be a very brave man to ask her whether she was going to make him a dad. He was brave, very brave, but he wasn't stupid.

"No, it was too big." She didn't see his look of disbelief, her eyes focussed on tucking her right hand out of sight.

"I don't believe you." The words escaping before he could stop them.

"I don't care what you believe." Her hand now wearily on her brow, brushing her hair back from her face.

"Now that I can believe!" He went to her then and, grabbing her wrists smoothed his fingers up over his ring before moving them towards her shoulders, her neck, her chin finally to turn her face to meet his.

"Why are we arguing, *ma chérie*?" he murmured softly, kissing her brow, her eyelids, her cheek, his words brushing against her lips. "Why are we arguing when all I want to do is this?" he added, caressing the blush pink skin, his hands cradling her in the gentlest embrace.

"But I don't want you to. I'm going to marry Rupert," pushing him away, her eyes huge in a face as pale as moonlight on a starlit night.

"But you can't, my darling," trying and failing to take her back into his arms.

"Why can't I?" Her eyes flashing. "Because the great Pascal de Sauvarin says so?" breath gasping out in spurts. "I'm going to marry

Rupert as soon as it can be arranged and live happily ever after."

"And what about us?" His hands dropping to his side, his face suddenly as pale as hers.

"Us, there is no us. There never was *any us*. I just…" Her eyes flickered briefly. "Rupert is so experienced and I wasn't. At least now I'll be able to enjoy my wedding night."

"You bitch!"

He never lost his temper, but now the heat coursing through his veins was so sudden, so unexpected that he had to clench his hands or risk placing them around her neck. "Why are you doing this? I know it's not true. What we had…"

"What we had, Pascal was a figment of your overtly French imagination. You men can have any women you want. Well, the shoe is on the other foot for a change. Yes, I'll admit I wanted you, if it will make you any happier." Her eyes insolent as she let them wander over his face, his chest, only to pause at his hips, his groin. "Just look at you, in fact I'd quite like a rematch but Rupert has forbidden it."

He turned away then, his eyes and then his feet moving to the door. He didn't know what to believe anymore. He'd been so sure; now he knew he'd never be sure of anything ever again. If she was telling the truth, if it had all been a lie, she'd left him nothing. His pride, his passion, his hopes, his dreams, his love all lay in tatters by her feet.

* * *

"There's something dreadfully wrong with Miss Sarah, Arnie."

"I know there is, luv but don't you go interfering now. She has to sort out her own life."

"But that handsome man in there." She paused, her arms up to their elbows in suds. "They love each other, I know they do and she's gone and gotten herself engaged to that prat."

"Bev, there's no good upsetting yourself."

"She doesn't know whether she's coming or going." Abandoning the sink and grabbing a tea-towel she turned to face him. "What's to become of her, married to that pompous...?"

"Now, now, pet, don't distress yourself. It'll all come out in the wash," he added, taking her hands in his and dropping a quick kiss on her forehead. His lips remained there as they both heard the slam of the lounge door and, turning to the window, watched as her visitor stormed off.

"Arnie," her eyes wide. "Go follow him. That's the least we can do. Offer him a lift or something? His lordship would want us to be civil to what could be his future son-in-law."

"What about the chickens?"

"What about them? Go on now, or you'll miss him," she said, shoving keys and phone into reluctant fingers as she pushed him towards the door.

Chapter Eleven

1st June. The worst types of liars are the ones that lie to themselves. Whatever my motives for sending him away I should have been able to come up with some sort of plan for us to be together. Now I'm going to have to put up with the consequences.

Sarah watched him go. She watched him go and her heart went with him. He'd called her a bitch; she was all that and more. But it was the only way if she wasn't going to saddle him with an unwanted child. It was the only way if either of them were to survive this mess. It was the only way…

Heading back to her bedroom she closed the blind against the glare of the June sunlight streaming through the window. She'd had enough of the world for now. Now she needed rest. But there was no rest to be had.

Her mind tumbled backwards and forwards over their conversation, her hand finding her stomach. Smoothing her palm over the still flat surface she tried to find some way out of her situation but all she could think about was running away.

She'd finally realised, standing there telling him all those lies that the one person she'd been lying to was herself. She couldn't disguise the fact she was pregnant with another man's child. She could have an abortion, her hand stilled before continuing its rhythmic massage. But she would never do that, her thumb curling up past her palm to feel the cool edge of his ring before removing it back to her left hand where it would stay.

She couldn't marry Rupert, she wouldn't marry him. Pascal was on his own with regards to his finances and so be it if her pictures were splattered across the gutter press.

Her eyes closed, her hand now a heavy weight of apology across her baby for her, albeit fleeting thoughts. She'd ask Mr Pidgeon about how best to break off the engagement, but not now; later, much later.

It was dark. She must have slept, slept for longer than she'd intended, her eyes finally adjusting to the blackness to make out the familiar shapes of her room. The rocking chair she'd had since a child and the wardrobe with its matching bedside cabinet. The pine bed with its pretty Laura Ashley covers, all comforting in their familiarity. And then there was the smell, the familiar smell of her father's Havana cigar.

Jumping out of bed, she raced to the door and, jerking it open, ran towards the lounge and straight into the arms of her dad.

Capturing her in a brief hug, he manoeuvred her back with a laugh. "And I'm pleased to see you too, but do mind my whiskey, won't you," he added, waving his Waterford glass high over her head.

"When did you get back? Why didn't you wake me?"

"Oh, hours ago, darling." It was her mother that answered, her father now settled in front of the television, trying to catch up with the football scores. "I popped my head in but you were sound asleep." Her mother, lounging back against the starkness of the leather surveyed her critically. "Rupert did say he'd kept you up late?"

"Yes, well…" But she was interrupted.

"We had the most marvellous time in St Tropez, darling. The Peters have a new 155 foot Sunseeker, it was glorious."

"I'm sure it was."

"And I was a little naughty," she twittered. "I bought you a few trifles for your trousseau from a delightful little lingerie shop along the *Rue Gambetta*."

"Mother, I don't need…"

"Oh yes you do. Rupert's a man of the world. He'll be expecting more than the tat you normally wear and there's nothing like a bit of satin and lace on your honeymoon."

"Yes Mother." Staring across at both her parents she suddenly wished she were anywhere else in the world. It was as if she wasn't even their daughter, her eyes glazing as her mother carried on discussing negligées and knickers. Perhaps she was a foundling after all, someone they'd found sitting on the doorstep along with their pint of milk. She loved them, of course she did. But at this moment, with her father grunting at the TV and her mother now discussing the gleaming steel and glass interior of the Peters new super ship, she finally realised they had nothing in common and they never would.

"I'm off to bed," she interrupted, bending over to place a kiss on her mother's perfumed cheek.

"But, darling." Her mother paused, suddenly noticing her pale face and heavy eyes. "You haven't eaten anything; the Hopper's have left you some soup…"

"I'm not hungry."

"Oh, all right then, but if you're no better in the morning, I'm phoning the doctor."

But sleep wouldn't come. Lying in the increasingly dark and silent house there was nothing to stop her from sleeping except her own thoughts, and they wouldn't leave her alone: her thoughts and then the pain. At first a niggly type of pain, just a cramp that would go away when she turned over only it didn't. Scared now; scared and alone she headed into the bathroom.

Although she'd expected it, the sight of blood seeping thought her knickers was a shock. The one thing that would get her out of her current situation was happening. The one thing, the very last thing she wanted, and all she could think about was her mother.

"Mum, wake up mum."

"Mmm, can't it wait till morning, darling." Her mother's only response.

"Mum, you must wake up. Please wake up," her voice dissolving into tears. "Mum, I need you."

Later, much later, found her lying against another bed, but this time the soft Laura Ashley bed set and down duvet swapped for harsh hospital linen and even harsher blankets. The doctor had gone, and the pain had been washed away by the drip pumping God only knew what into her right arm. She wouldn't let them use her left arm, she wouldn't let them remove her ring. Hopper had called the ambulance while Beverley, dear kind Beverley, had gathered everything she might need and her parents; her parents started questioning her.

"Food poisoning? Appendicitis? When did you last eat?"

"Oh for Heaven's sake! I'm pregnant."

"Pregnant, but I thought Rupert had the snip after he'd had the fourth?"

"Don't be so thick, Mother."

"Oh you mean it's not…" Her eyes wide. "It's that Frenchman, isn't it? Oh poor Rupert, he's going to be so upset."

She eased her shoulders off the trolley the kindly ambulance man had just helped her on to. "He doesn't need to know I'm…"

"You're father's already phoned him." She caught her daughter's look of reproof. "Well we thought you had food poisoning, and you are engaged to him after all."

"I'm breaking it off."

"You're what?"

"Mother, I can't marry him, all right. It wouldn't be fair to either of us."

"I suppose not. I hope he doesn't sue you for breach of promise."

"Let him try, it hasn't been formally announced in The Times yet."

"That's true." She shook her head in near disbelief. "I thought I'd brought you up better than that, darling. Couldn't you have used one of those rubber thingies?"

"Mother! It's bad enough having to tell you I'm pregnant, let alone you advising me about my love life."

"What about the Frenchman, Pascal? Did you want me to…?"

"On no circumstances are you to phone him. I forbid it." Her eyes wild in her face.

* * *

Pulling into the hospital car park on a screech of tyres, he abandoned the taxi at a run, pressing a bundle of scrunched up notes into the alarmed taxi driver's hand as he raced across the tarmac, leather jacket flying open behind him.

Please let her be all right. Please let her be all right. Please let her…

The repeating mantra had reverberated around and around his head ever since the phone call. He'd been just about to pay his hotel bill in time to catch the first flight back to Charles de Gauille when the bottle blonde receptionist, squeezed into something at least six sizes too small, held out the hotel phone to him.

He'd nearly refused to take it for surely it must be a mistake? No one knew he was here. No one knew where he was staying and much less cared. Looking at the phone in horror he finally lifted it to his ear, his mind in turmoil as he suddenly remembered being persuaded to accept a lift back up to town by Hopper. Hopper knew, only Hopper: Hopper who in some ways reminded him of his uncle, with his stiff manner concealing a kind heart.

He must have handed the phone back after hearing the news. He must have remembered to pay his bill and even pick up his rucksack and find a taxi. He must have sat in the back, retracing the same journey for the third time in two days but he could remember none of it. All he could think about was the same line repeating itself over and over again.

Please let her be all right.

He wasn't allowed see her. He wasn't allowed to have his questions answered. He was allowed nothing.

"I'm sorry, and you are? Oh you're a nobody, not even a friend. It's family only at the moment. No, I can't tell you how she's doing, after all you're not important are you…? In fact you're nothing, a nonentity just cluttering up my pristine white corridor and

making it messy. There's a coffee machine over there, if you can be bothered, and don't ask for any change because even if I had any I wouldn't give it to you. And your accent; it's not English. French is it? I would have said Austrian. I went there on holiday once; Salzburg, wonderful bread. Come along now, no dawdling, I don't have all day, Blah blah blah," her words slamming into his head as she directed him to a small waiting room with hideous orange chairs and naff paintings of cloudless summer days.

He watched her retreating back, her bottom huge in oversized scrubs. He would have laughed but he couldn't. It seemed he'd have to wait for her family to arrive, the people who loved her the most. Well, that was a joke for a start, his hand flicking through a copy of Country Life, four years out of date.

He felt his stomach rumble but he couldn't eat. He'd be sick if he ate, his eyes wandering over to the drinks machine in the corner. He shuddered as he remembered the last time he'd been foolish enough to purchase coffee from a drinks machine. However desperate he was for caffeine he was never that desperate. Closing his eyes against the harsh lighting he tried and failed to reach any degree of comfort from the tacky, stained plastic chair; his mind, his body, his soul with her in the room at the end of the corridor.

"What are you doing here?"

The voice, overly harsh, overly loud or was it just because he'd drifted off into a semi-dreamlike state, the only way he could shut down his thoughts. It was shut them down or go mad. Snapping his eyes open he found himself being glared at by Rupert, and forced himself to smile.

"*Bonjour* Rupert."

"Don't you *bonjour* me, sonny - I asked you a question?"

"I'm here to see Sarah, why else?"

"How did you know…?"

"Well, if she didn't tell you…?"

"Don't be cheeky," his eyes glinting. "Especially as you're the reason she's in here."

He felt cold where seconds before he'd been too hot in the overly stuffy room.

His fault, how could it be his fault? He'd done nothing. His eyes, now glued to Rupert's self-satisfied face, his mind shifting back over what he knew. What had Hopper said? He'd said nothing, only that she was ill, and they'd had to get an ambulance.

He wouldn't ask him what he knew; he wouldn't give him that satisfaction. By the look on his face he was going to tell him anyway.

"Ha, that's floored you. You smarmy French git with your flattery and flowery words. You might have been able to talk her into bed. What was it, made her drunk did you? You'd have had to have given her something," as he looked at the scruffy jeans and vintage bomber jacket. "Men like you make me sick. Screwing her brains out and then leaving without a thought for her afterwards. What did you come back for anyway? To have another go at her? Well the damage was done the first time. Just go away and leave her to those who actually love her," he finished, slumping into the chair opposite before picking up the same copy of Country Life and burying his head amongst the pages.

"I. I," his voice low as he struggled to retain even a semblance of calm. In truth all he wanted to do was pick him up and smash his head against the wall until he dragged the truth out of him. He glanced down at his hands curling into fists and he imagined pummelling his knuckles into all that soft flabby flesh. But hitting him wouldn't solve anything and he was pretty sure that nurse would kick him out – and then what? He'd have no way of finding out the truth. He'd told him nothing, nothing he could fix on, he thought, his eyes riveted to his bent head. She was ill because of him. He'd made her ill.

Oh my God, his gaze flickering towards the door. *She must be pregnant.*

He only turned back at the sound of Rupert's voice.

"If she'd only come and told me," his attention seemingly focussed on the details of an Eighteenth-Century farmhouse with indoor pool. "But no, she was too proud. Instead of letting me arrange an abortion, she had to go to some backstreet centre and now..," the catch clear in his voice. "And now she's in there bleeding to dea..."

He'd had enough. Pushing himself up to standing he watched as Rupert turned the page and started to examine a modern take on a shaker style kitchen somewhere in the Welsh valleys.

Pregnant? Abortion? She couldn't. She wouldn't, would she? But then again how would he know what she'd do. He didn't know her. In the few short hours they'd been together they'd never really talked about the future, about kids. He knew she was scared but then that was understandable given her history. As for him, he wanted them. He wanted them desperately, but only with her, and now...

The nurse was at the door, all smiles but only for Rupert.

"Your fiancée will see you now, Mr Reynolds-Smythe. She's over the worst, but you can only have five minutes."

There was nothing for him, not even a look in his direction, but he knew there wouldn't be. Sarah wouldn't want to see him now. She wouldn't want to see him again and he couldn't blame her. Rupert was right. If he hadn't thrown himself at her she wouldn't be at death's door. He'd known she was untouched, despite that newspaper article. It had been his responsibility, and he'd let himself down, he'd let her down, and now; and now they'd both have to live with the consequences.

As soon as Rupert sauntered through the door he collected his belongings, his movements slow where before they'd been quick. He'd missed his plane, but that didn't matter. Paris held no attraction now she wasn't there. Walking towards the main entrance he didn't see Rupert storming out of the room, closely followed by the twittering nurse. He didn't see anything apart from the bleakness of the future that lay ahead.

Chapter Twelve

14ᵗʰ June. After weeks of lassitude I've finally moved on with my life. There are still decisions to be made, like what I'm going to do with the next sixty years or so but they'll have to wait until after my birthday.

"But darling…"

"There's no but's Mother. I'm not having a big party. After all, what do I have to celebrate?" she said, her voice determined as she folded the selection of clothes she'd laid out across the bed. "It's only a birthday."

"Darling, you wouldn't reconsider Rupert's proposal? All that lovely money."

"Even after he tried to destroy me with those photographs, mother? How could you?"

"Your father's dealt with all that as you very well know. It was just a huge misunderstanding…"

"Yeah. Right! He only handed over the negatives when he realised it would affect his business dealings with daddy. He doesn't care for me. He doesn't love me and I absolutely hate him. For the very last time, I wouldn't marry Rupert if he looked like…"

"Looks aren't everything; take me and your father."

"You're not that bad looking, Mother," her smile ingenuous.

"Sarah, be serious," she interrupted, peering in the mirror at her near perfect complexion and gym toned body with a look of inquiry and then a smile. "What about that handsome French man?"

"He hasn't been in touch."

"I know, and that does surprise me."

"How so?" Sarah's hand paused, mid-fold before placing the last of her skirts on top of the case.

"He was at the hospital."

"When? When was he at the hospital? You never said?"

"Well, we didn't want to upset you. That sweet nurse, you know; the one with the large bottom?"

"Mary?"

"Yes, that's right, Mary. She said something to your father."

"But how would he have known?" She watched as her mother shrugged her shoulders.

"Beats me, I didn't even know he was in the country," eyeing her daughter with a knowing look.

"He visited me the day you got back."

"The same day you…?"

"Yes Mother, that's right. The same day I…" Slamming her case shut with a snap. "Look, do we really have to discuss all this now? It's ancient history."

"If you say so," smoothing a pleat in her brand new, cream Victoria Beckham skirt. "I take it he doesn't know about the baby?"

"No, and I'm not going to tell him."

"Have it your own way darling, but he does have a right to know," she said, standing up and tweaking her daughter's ponytail before changing the subject. "Are you sure you'll be able to manage on the salary, £200 a week isn't very much?"

"Mother, I'll manage, after all I've nothing to spend it on. I'll be living in."

"The thought of my daughter working as a nanny." She shook her head in dismay.

"They do have a peerage, and it is only for a couple of weeks until they return to Canada."

"It's the only thing that made your father agree to your silly scheme."

"I am twenty-two…"

"And soon to be a very poor twenty-three-year old; don't remind me!" she said, smoothing back Sarah's hair from her face.

Hopper dropped her off outside the impressive, six story property in Belgravia with a sigh.

"You will keep in touch, Sarah? You know how we worry."

"Of course I will, Arnie," she said, hugging him briefly before ringing the bell on the highly polished black door with a nervous hand.

The advert in The Lady for a short term French speaking nanny had her reaching for the phone and, on hearing of her impeccable credentials, they agreed to hire her on the spot. Sarah still wasn't quite sure whether it was her time at the Sorbonne or her title that swung it, probably the latter, but whatever the reason, from tomorrow she was taking sole charge of the daughter of the house.

The terraced house along Eaton Square was impressive with a winding central staircase to rival that of Cosgrave Manor, but where the manor had its feet firmly stuck in the past, Lord and Lady Clivveley's London residence was straight out of Vogue. Everything from the stainless steel staircase with French mezzanine internal balconies around the central auditorium to the bleached white woods screamed modern and money; lots and lots of money.

A French maid, dressed in something you'd normally find in a fancy dress shop opened the door and led her directly into the drawing room where, presumably, the lady of the house languished on an ornate chaise longue.

"There you are at last," she said, offering a limp hand. "Meg will have your luggage sent up to your room directly. We've given you the room next to the nursery. Lady Kylie gets terribly nervous in the dark, and I do so like not being disturbed."

So much for a good night's sleep, but Sarah just smiled. She was here to work after all, to work and forget if that was possible. So be it if she was up half the night, it didn't really matter.

"I'll send tea up. We eat at eight, but I'll get Meg to have something sent up on a tray," Lady Clivveley said, ringing the little brass hand bell by her side.

"Ah Meg, if you can show Lady Sarah to her room, and..." she paused, her cool grey eyes staring at her. "A reminder that this is a French speaking household."

The first week flew by. The nursery was everything she'd expected, filled to the brim with an assortment of toys presumably ordered in from Hamley's. All the books were in French and even the TV could only get French channels, not that she had much time to watch it.

Her day started early with a cup of tea brought up at 6 am. Her wake-up alarm, she called it as it just gave her enough time to shower and scrabble into her clothes before Lady Kylie bounced into her room with a mouthful of chatter that needed her undivided attention. She'd sort of lied about the fluent in French part but talking to the little girl was a delight and she'd soon expanded her vocabulary to include keywords like hairbands, scrunchies and teddy bears.

As it was now June she spent most mornings exploring the parks with pockets-full of seeds for the ducks and her blonde-haired, blue-eyed companion proved an ideal distraction from her troubles. She had an hour free after lunch when Kylie rested on her little, pink, canopied princess bed, but she didn't leave the house. Instead she stole away with a book to sit in a quiet spot in the handkerchief sized garden pretending to read, all her thoughts on Pascal and what they'd lost.

Her time here was like a dream, a dream where she'd been whisked away from everything and everybody she knew to live a very different kind of life. She'd got used to being ignored by everyone in the house except for Kylie and the other servants, because in this household that's exactly what she was.

After that first day she wasn't allowed to use the main entrance and had to keep her presence in the front hall to a minimum lest any of the frequent guests found themselves mingling amongst the wall-to-wall marble with one of the lower classes.

Closing her eyes against the glare of the sun, she couldn't prevent a giant smirk for, of course, Lord Clivveley's title was only bestowed and not inherited like her father's. She'd Googled them earlier in the week, her eyes dancing when she'd learnt he'd earned his title because he was something big in soap and as for his wife, her giggle turning into a snort. He'd met her on a photo shoot in Quebec where she'd dared to bare all in a bath full of his deluxe bath crystals. But, of course, that was a long time ago. Now they consorted with minor royalty in addition to expanding their range to include toothpaste and toilet rolls.

As long as they didn't come up to the nursery and pong the place out with heavy handed perfume, she didn't really care that she had to speak French. Tomorrow was her birthday, which made today her last day and then - she hadn't thought about "and then," but she didn't really have to. Tomorrow, instead of being heiress to a fortune, she'd be the girl who'd just thrown away eighty million because she could. Tomorrow a huge weight would be lifted, and she'd be just like any other working woman trying to earn a crust. Her hand dropped her book to the ground as she allowed her palm to rest on the gentle swell of her stomach, a silent tear finding its way down her cheek.

With her hour's rest long since past, she was now curled up beside her charge for wind down time and she just knew which cartoon Lady Kylie would choose.

"Sarah, Sarah, Peppa Pig. *Je veux* Peppa Pig."

"*D'accord, ma petite.*" Anything for a quiet life, she added silently as she switched on the wall mounted TV and pressed play.

It didn't matter just how many times Lady Kylie watched the antics of Peppa Pig, that's still all she wanted to watch; over and over again. So instead of having to watch Grandpa Pig trundling up the hill she picked up her phone and scrolled through until she found the one new message, an early birthday congratulations from Cara. They were just about back on their usual easy footing after falling out briefly over the baby and, with her friend flying back for her birthday, there'd be lots of catching up to do.

There was no news apart from the happiness of others so she snapped her phone closed and turned back to her thoughts with a sigh. She'd been hoping against hope he'd at least text her, although why she should expect anything after the way she'd spoken to him? She deserved nothing, and that's what she was getting: nothing.

She felt Kylie's hand weave through hers and she gave it a little squeeze.

"You shouldn't be sad on your birthday, Sarah."

"Ah, but it's not my birthday until tomorrow, *petite*."

"I've got you a present, Meg helped me to wrap it but it's a secret," she added, holding up a chubby finger to her lips.

"A secret between you and me, poppet." She drew her into a brief hug. "I'll open it tomorrow before I leave. Now, time for bath and bed, and if you're really good, I'll read you two stories."

"Can I choose them?" Her china-blue eyes wide.

"*Certainement*."

After two Peppa Pig stories, snugged up under the duvet, she gave her a brief kiss on her forehead before switching on the little Peppa Pig bedside light.

Tonight wasn't one of the nights her parents deigned to walk up that final flight to the top floor to give their beloved daughter a goodnight kiss, something Kylie never referred to but it hurt her all the same. It was there in the half shut gaze staring relentlessly at the door. It was there in the hug that was more of a stranglehold. It was there in the whispered good night and the way she turned her back. It was there and, other than racing down the stairs to drag them up by the scruff of their stinky necks, there was nothing she could do about it apart from love her a little bit more.

Heading back to the nursery she noticed Meg had left her supper on the little table under the window. She wasn't hungry but, picking up the fork she started working her way through the prettily presented mushroom omelette.

There was no enjoyment. She ate because she had to, just like she had to drink and just like she had to breathe to live. Pleasure was primarily a thing of the past. It only lingered at the edges, glimmering like a fragile sunset only to fade and then die into the perpetual blackness that was becoming as familiar as a friend.

Ignoring the sherry trifle, she picked up her coffee before heading back to the sofa. The room, silent apart from the gentle ticking of the clock was a sharp reminder that apart from the company of a precocious five year old, she was primarily alone; alone and lonely.

She missed home, she missed Paris but most of all she missed him. She didn't know how or even why but there it was. She couldn't even list what exactly it was that made him so special; special to her. It didn't matter. Whatever he may have felt, and it was probably very little, there was no way he'd ever try to see her after the way she'd treated him. So, instead of having to put up with her thoughts she flicked on the television in an effort to forget.

She didn't know what she wanted to watch, in truth as long as it didn't contain any pigs, real or imaginary, she'd be happy. With her cup perched on her lap she scrolled through the channels, finally pausing on the news in some kind of desperation. There were too many programmes to choose from, too many programmes about things she wasn't interested in. It was a toss-up between the news or cricket and the news won.

The news couldn't hold her attention but she watched all the same while waiting for the weather report. With her luck, the glorious flaming June sunshine would be obliterated by black cloud and thunderstorms. At the moment she wouldn't be surprised if Belgravia was struck by an unseasonal snowstorm or even a tornado.

The grim smile pulling at her lips froze as the tornado struck but not the one she'd been waiting for. She hadn't been listening, not really. She had little interest in French politics and the last item was a small one, slipped in presumably as a stopgap between the news and the weather.

And finally the police are increasingly concerned for the whereabouts of the Marquis de Sauvarin. The acclaimed architect is still missing despite concerted efforts by both the French and English police. The six foot three, dark-haired businessman failed to return to Paris following a trip to London four weeks ago.

Her eyes glazed as she tried to focus on the switchover to their reporter in Paris and she missed almost all of the thirty second interview with Rexi, now dressed up in a dark grey suit instead of his regulation denim cut-offs and black beanie.

Missing, how the hell could he be missing? She fumbled with the end of her ponytail as she tried to puzzle it out. The last sighting was when he'd checked out of his hotel on the first of June, the morning after she'd arrived in hospital. A frown pierced her brow. There'd been something wrong with the report, something she couldn't quite work out. But her phone rang, interrupting her musings and scattering her thoughts like leaves on a windy day.

"Darling, I've just been watching the news with your father."

"So have I, Mother. Well, not with Father, but you know what I mean."

"I'm most disappointed in you darling…"

"What?" She held the phone away briefly before returning it to her ear. "What the hell have I done to disappoint you? My…" She stuttered to a halt. She'd been about to call him her boyfriend but he wasn't that, he wasn't really a friend, certainly not after the way she'd treated him. "He's missing, Mother. He might even be dead."

"Let's be positive darling. He's probably gone off in a huff; Rupert isn't known for his diplomacy."

Rupert, of course! Rupert had been the last person to see him. That's what had been puzzling her. The report had been wrong.

"Rupert was the last one to see him, he wouldn't surely…" her voice a whisper as her imagination took over and came up with the inevitable conclusion.

"No, he wouldn't. Rupert's many things but a murderer?" She gave a little laugh. "You did upset him terribly, but I hear he's dating a Texan heiress now."

"So, he's not that upset then." She smiled, despite the bottom having dropped out of her heart.

"Why didn't you tell us, Sarah? Your father is most upset."

"Tell you what?"

"About him being a Marquis, silly."

"A Marquis?" She faltered, "I thought that was some kind of tent?"

"Very funny! Your father wants you to contact him, there's still time for you to get engaged."

"Haven't you been listening? He's missing, possibly dead and you're wittering on about me becoming engaged to a what: a corpse," her voice shaking. "And anyway I'd be the last person in the world he'd think of marrying; not now!" She stared at the phone in silence even as her mother's tinny voice continued to shout back at her.

"Dead, he's not dead. He's gone away to lick his wounds. He must love you very much."

"Must he? I hurt him so badly."

"What, a tough bloke like him? Hardly. You might have bruised his ego a little but he'll bounce back. Now we don't have much time, Sarah. Where do you think he's holed up?"

"How on earth should I know? He could be anywhere?"

"Mmm, that is a problem."

"Mother, do you really think he still loves me?"

"I really do. He reminds me a little of your father you know; when we split up."

"You split up?" Her eye widened. "You never told me?"

"It was all a very long time ago, darling, before we were even engaged. He disappeared for a month over some silly red roses I'd received. He eventually returned with his tail between his legs and a sapphire the size of Gibraltar."

"And what about the roses?"

"Oh, ahem, well. You know your father, he's not the most romantic, so I, er, sent them to myself."

"Mother, did you ever tell him?"

"No and don't you go…"

"My lips are sealed." She tried and failed to suppress the giggle bubbling inside at the thought of her *stiff-upper-lipped* dad being managed so very well. The giggle faded to nothing as her memory flicked back to the cream rose she'd pressed between the pages of one of her heavier music books. She'd never have that problem with Pascal; if only she could find him. If only he wasn't dead.

Tucking up her legs she finally let go of her hair and allowed both hands grip the phone. "Where is he? Why would he go into hiding like that?"

"Well I think he's waiting it out."

"Waiting what out?"

"Sarah, I know you're all loved up but get your brain into gear. He's waiting until after your birthday, which is such a bloody waste." She heard her heave a sigh and smiled. Her mother was so predictable. "He probably expects to see your engagement to Rupert in The Times…"

Would he? Yes, of course he would, if he loved her. So he was either lying in some ditch or waiting until she wasn't an heiress anymore. Staring into the middle distance a grin started to pull at her lips even as she heard her mother screaming down the phone.

"Darling, are you still there…?"

"Mother, I have a plan."

"Good, at last! Spit it out then, darling?"

"Do you remember the name of that horrible reporter, the one who did that splash on me and my Sax?"

"P.P. Latrine?"

"That's it! I knew it was something stupid."

"Darling, if you're going to do what I think you are, it's a very mean trick. He may never forgive you."

"If you can think of another way to flush him out in time for my birthday..?"

"Oh, very funny! Flush him out is it! Okay darling, but don't say I didn't warn you."

Chapter Thirteen

1ˢᵗ July. It's her birthday, not that it feels like her birthday.

It feels like the worst day of my life. I feel as if I've lost everything, everything that's of any importance with the shifting of the calendar from one day to the next. Yesterday there was hope; now there is no hope.

"Ah there you are, hen. I've got a nice wee potato cake and some of that black pudding you're so fond of. You just sit yourself by the window and admire the view. I'll be back in a tick."

"Er, thank you, Mrs McCloud."

"The newspapers have just arrived by the front desk if you'd like to…?"

"No, I don't think so, maybe later." he added, managing a brief smile as he spread his tartan napkin across his lap. He'd have to see the newspapers: newspapers he'd been avoiding for the last four weeks, just as he'd been ignoring his phone. In fact, spacing his knife and fork wider, it wasn't just his phone or the news he'd been deliberately avoiding, it was life itself.

He could barely remember the first few hours after he'd left the hospital. He found himself at a railway station asking for a single for the train pulling into the station, which happened to be the 10:10 to Aberdeen. He couldn't quite recall where that was, but it didn't matter, nothing really mattered anymore. Using his rucksack as a pillow he must have slept. Before he knew it, the train had pulled into Glasgow's Queen Street Station where, apparently, he had to change. Looking about at the heaving platform he'd nearly turned on his heel, and he probably would have except for a fat woman in florals poking him in the back with her tartan walking stick.

Why was he even here when he could be by her side? But she didn't want him, she didn't want his child; their child as he headed into Starbucks and automatically ordered a double espresso to go. There was no point in anything anymore, he thought, cradling his cup in hands as cold as the expression on her face the last time he'd seen her. Was it only yesterday? Was it only yesterday she'd sent him away? He didn't know. He didn't know anything anymore as he started on the next leg of his journey.

He didn't sleep now, he wanted to but, placing his bag by his feet, his mind, his heart wouldn't let him. Like the view screaming past his window, he recalled the first time he'd seen her. The sense of wonder, surprise even that, at last he'd found her. He'd found something, someone he didn't even know he was looking for.

"There's a fine thing, laddie, on the front of the newspaper, which you may like to read," her eyes twinkling.

"Yes, Mrs McCloud?" He glanced up from the pile of toast she obviously thought he needed. In truth he felt sick, but she'd be offended if he didn't at least make some sort of an effort.

She'd looked after him better than any mother could ever look after her son; a stranger who'd landed on the doorstop of the Ship Inn with only a rucksack to his name. He wasn't even sure where he was. Stonehaven was delightfully pretty and quiet so he'd stayed because he hadn't anywhere better to go. He'd only planned on staying a couple of days in the best front room they had but days had quickly turned into weeks and before he knew it he'd been here a month, a whole month and today was the day he'd been dreading.

"Yes, that heiress, you know the one. Lady Sarah Cosgrave. Oh are you all right, laddie?"

He'd dropped the marmalade at the sound of her name, a name he hadn't heard in weeks except in the dark recesses of his mind. He didn't see the glass dish roll onto the floor, bouncing along the highly polished parquet with a clatter before landing the right way up with a final dull thud. He didn't see her grab a cloth and start mopping up the globs of orange gloop splattered in a starburst formation; all he saw was Sarah.

Finally he managed to shake himself back to the present and went to help.

"No, no you just sit there and I'll bring you some…"

"No, I'm fine, more than fine," he interrupted, patting his stomach. "You'll be making me fat."

"What, a great big hulk of a man like you? Shush away with you now and I'll be bringing you back some more toast, and what about a few potato cakes?" she paused, suddenly awkward; her gaze flickering wildly from side to side. "Er, I shouldn't be calling you laddie, you being a Marquis and all."

Folding his napkin, he stood up and placed a light kiss against her cheek. "Laddie is just fine, in fact," he added. "I prefer it."

He wanted to ask how she knew but he was pretty sure he was about to find out. "It's been a great holiday, but it's about time I went back to France." He smiled down at her pink cheeks. "If you could let me have the bill, I'm sure to be back."

Picking up the newspaper from the front desk he strolled across to the beach opposite before dropping on to the slipway, his feet dangling over the side. He'd rolled the paper into a tube and now, the thought of unfurling the words he knew would greet him on the front page was almost too much to bear. Heaving a sigh, he twisted the paper until it mangled in front of him before unfolding it. He didn't need to see the print to know what it said, but somehow he couldn't prevent himself from lowering his gaze to the headlines.

Staring at the words in almost disbelief, his hands smoothed over the picture of Sarah, the same picture he stared at every night before curling up and trying to sleep.

The whereabouts of the Marquis de Sauvarin are of increasing concern. His fiancée, Lady Sarah Cosgrave..."

He didn't read anymore, he couldn't. Scrunching up the paper into a ball he flung it into the nearest bin and headed back to the guesthouse at a run.

Chapter Fourteen

1st July. It's my birthday, not that it feels like my birthday. It feels like the worst day of my life. I look the part in my designer dress and designer shoes but I don't feel the part. I feel as if I've lost everything; everything that's of any importance.

It was the early evening now, and she was back at Cosgrave Manor sitting under the shade of the weeping willow that pierced the side lawn like a palm tree marking a desert island. This was her place, the place she'd always come as a child, at first chewing the end of a pencil as she puzzled over her algebra. Then, older as she'd hidden away with one of the books her mother used to squirrel under her mattress. She'd even carved a few initials into the bark only to hack at them as she tried to change the letters like some reject trying to eradicate the tattoo of a former lover. Now she sat still, her bare feet stretched out, a pair of high-heel, midnight blue stilettos beside her. Her dress was midnight blue to match, almost the colour of her eyes. But it wasn't the fifties style, wide silk skirt she stared at but her ring, his ring as it flickered brightly in the light of the gently fading sun.

It was the early evening, and he hadn't phoned; he hadn't texted, he hadn't emailed. It seemed as if the rest of England; no, the world, had been in touch and, wherever she looked all she saw was his face butted up next to hers like those wanted criminal notices on Crime Watch.

She was losing hope, her hands resting across her lap, her eyes closed. She should be happy, gloriously happy. She was officially engaged and now the organiser of her own destiny. She had the money to do whatever she wanted, but without him it was a hollow victory, without him her life was dust.

Looking up her eyes slid to the marquee as she remembered just how miffed her father had been earlier. He'd probably been the most miffed she'd ever seen him when he'd told her over afternoon tea that a Marquis was higher up in the Royalty rankings than a mere Earl. Gobbling like a chicken she watched in silent amusement as he continued wittering on as they munched their way through cucumber sandwiches and scones about the likelihood of having to bow to his own son-in-law.

It would be funny if it wasn't so bloody tragic.

Where was he?

The party was small; intimate friends and family coming together to celebrate her good fortune in actually managing to become engaged just in time for her twenty-third birthday. She wasn't in the mood to celebrate her birthday, just as she wasn't in the mood to celebrate her mess of a life. She was alone and pregnant, not to mention being in possession of a fortune she had no entitlement to. What was there to celebrate?

So Instead of celebrating, she hovered on the edge, refusing any offers to dance while she watched and waited.

She heard the whispers flowing around her like a rampant rash as to the whereabouts of the missing groom-to-be. She heard the sudden silences as she moved into hearing range but she ignored them all. They weren't really here to see her anyway and, apart from Cara huddled in the corner with Aaron, she'd be quite happy for them all to disappear in a puff of smoke. Her eyes snagged on Rupert: Rupert in a ridiculous tie and with a ridiculous girlfriend. He'd gone from one extreme to the other. This one old enough to be his mother, but a very rich mother who'd seen off at least two very wealthy husbands, She wondered, with the sliver of a smile whether he'd be husband number three.

Her parents had gone to a lot of trouble and even now were holding court, a bottle of champagne open in front of them. She'd played their game. She'd played at eating the food Beverley had prepared and she'd admired the giant cake made in the shape of her sax, but that was all. Now, with a headache pressing behind her eyes, she had to escape. No one would miss her now; now she'd cut the cake like some blushing bride minus the bridegroom, which was exactly how she felt. Wherever he was - he wasn't here.

Heading outside, she felt the cool breeze lift her hair off her face even as her shoes sank into the freshly mown grass. Kicking them off and allowing the soft turf embrace the soles of her feet was the first real pleasure she'd had today. The grass felt slightly damp now the sky had turned from blue, red and then finally to black. She'd probably end up with green feet, she thought on a laugh, but green feet were the least of her worries.

Those same feet took her towards her tree; her sanctuary, her escape for if she headed back towards the house they'd be sure to find her. She didn't want to be found, she didn't want people, she didn't want anyone or anything; only him.

She'd reached the tree now and, raising her hand to the firm, almost black wood ran her hands over the names she'd carved into the bark earlier, the flesh strangely white in the glimmering light cast from the fairy lights Hopper had streamed between the branches. Wrapping her arms around the trunk she sank her forehead against the timber almost in despair; this engraving was all she had left to mark their romance.

"*Bonjour,* Sarah."

She heard the words, but only in her head and thought she was going mad. She must be mad, her eyes following the curls and grooves of the bark only millimetres from her lashes. She heard the words and then she felt his hands on her shoulders as he turned her round to face him, but she couldn't look. She'd open her eyes, and he'd be gone. It had happened before, it was happening again. Squeezing her eyes tight she felt hands move up to span her face and then pressure as his lips touched hers. A groan escaped; a deep plaintive sound as she was still unable to believe what her hammering heart was trying to tell her.

"Sarah, *ma chérie.*"

He was kissing her forehead, her eyelids, her cheek, even her chin before tilting it up. "Look at me Sarah, after all, we are engaged, although I seem to have forgotten the proposal?"

She blushed, the heat coursing up her cheeks even as she pulled away. "We're not actually engaged," she mumbled, only to be interrupted.

"*Au contraire, ma petite*." His hand fumbling for hers as he raised the ring to his lips. "You're wearing my ring after all."

"Pascal, I was desperate."

"*D'accord*, that will of your aunt's. Well, I'm pleased to have been of use." He stepped back, his eyes glinting in the darkness. "So, what are you going to spend all your money on then because, when we're married you'll be spending mine?"

"Money? Yours? What?"

"It's quite simple, Sarah. I'm quite able to afford a wife, even one with expensive tastes like yours." His eyes flickering over her dress with a look she didn't like.

"This was a present from my parents," her hand floating to the neck of her low-cut gown.

"And very charming it is too, but in future I'll be buying your clothes."

"Well, I need some new knickers so next time you're in town if you wouldn't mind…"

"Don't push me, Lady Sarah," a muscle flickering along his jaw." I'm not some Rupert to be trifled with. You can buy whatever you want," his eyes brushing over her cleavage.

"Especially if it's for my benefit. So how is Rupert?"

Her eyes widened at the change of topic. "Rupert?"

"Yes, Rupert; that tosspot of a former lover."

"He was never my lover."

"No, perhaps not," he said, raking his hand through his hair, his eyes now on her stomach. "Let's not argue, it's the last thing I want to do. I couldn't bear the thought of you with him," his voice dwindling to a whisper as he gently pulled her down on the ground to cradle her on his lap, his hands smoothing themselves over the planes of her body.

"I'd never have married Rupert." She stared across the lawn to the marquee framed in the distance, the muffled tones of some dance tune or other just audible in the distance.

"So when do you want to get married then, I believe it's the bride's prerogative to choose?"

Something wasn't right. She'd been dreaming of this night for so long and now… and now he seemed different, alien almost.

"Pascal?"

"Mmm?" His voice soft as he continued tracing his hands up and down her arms.

"Pascal, I have something to tell you."

"It's all right my love, I forgive you. I'm sure Rupert put you up to it, anyway."

"What?" She would have scrabbled off his lap, only his arms, so gentle had turned to bands of steel even as he started trailing a line of kisses across her skin.

"I said I forgive you. It hurt at the time, it hurt dreadfully but I'm good now."

"Pascal, what are you talking about?"

His mouth stilled, his lips vibrating the words against her neck. "I don't really want to talk about it."

Taking advantage of his slightly looser grip she moved away and he let her, his hands now by his side, his look wary.

Hands on hips, she stared down at him, her face pale in the darkness. "Why the hell do you think I'm in need of forgiveness; because I wasn't on the pill, because I allowed you to…?" Her voice broke, her fingers struggling in vain to pull off the ring.

"Shush Sarah, calm down. It's all right now, everything will be all right. We can have more children; we can fill the house with as many babies as you can find room for."

"Why would I want more children?" Her hand moving to the gentle swell of her stomach, just visible now she'd smoothed her dress against her skin. "What's wrong with the one I've got; the one we made in Paris?"

It was his turn to look pale. She wouldn't have believed the sickly pallor if she hadn't seen for herself the way the colour leached out of his face. "But Rupert said."

"Rupert said?" she queried softly. Where before she'd felt anger, intense unexplainable anger at the man in front of her, now all she felt was love, a deep all-encompassing love. She watched him turn away, his hands hiding his face and suddenly she knew. She knew what Rupert would have said to hurt him the most. She knew what had made him run away.

"You were in hospital, Hopper called."

"I was bleeding. It can happen apparently, but I wasn't to know that. I thought I was losing our child, so I panicked."

Kneeling beside him she pulled his hands away before wiping the tears streaking down his face and then, turning his palm upwards gently placed it over their baby. "It's a little too soon to feel him or her move but to answer your question: soon."

"Soon?"

"Soon, I'd like to be married soon, before this little person turns me into an elephant, although," her eyes sparkling as she placed both hands on his shoulders and pulled him forward on to his knees. "I do think you should propose, in fact I won't marry you until you do."

"But, but," his sudden frown stilling her fingers. "What about you? What about that medical condition. I didn't think you wanted to risk getting pregnant?"

"Well, it's all a bit late for that, don't you think? And anyway," she added gently. "My mother has had me up and down Harley Street to see some supposed expert. I can't blink and they take my blood pressure." Leaning back she ran her hands through his hair before grabbing a lock and giving it a quick tug. "So, *Monsieur Builder?*"

"So, Lady Sarah, will you marry me?" his voice tender as he withdrew an envelope out of his pocket.

"Of course I will," her attention now riveted on the piece of paper he was slowly unfolding with all the panache of a magician's final reveal. "What's that?"

"It's a special licence, *ma chérie*," holding up the decidedly battered-looking document. "It's a special licence that I've been carrying around now for a month. Your parents didn't by any chance invite Uncle George to the ceremony did they? I thought we could save them the expense of another party?"

Epilogue

2nd July, The morning after the night before. Pascal promised me the most amazing honeymoon in the most amazing place imaginable. In return I have a few little surprises up my sleeve. Well, in truth only one but it's worth millions!

"All right, Hen, and it's a lovely day, so it is. Now what will it be for you both, the full Scottish? I've a pot of porridge too or a few kippers?" Mrs McCloud continued her breakfast litany as she fussed over the table, making sure the cutlery was just so.

They'd arrived late yesterday afternoon to be greeted by a traditional Scottish afternoon tea complete with smoked salmon and shortbread, and now with their wedding night under their belt they looked forward to continuing their gourmet break at the hands of what must be the best cook in all of Scotland.

As soon as she'd disappeared with their order, he leant across the table to press a deep kiss on already bruised lips. "A week of this and I'll have to go on a diet," his hand wandering under the table and gently massaging their baby. "At least you've got an excuse."

"Stop it," she laughed, grabbing his hand and placing it on her knee as a pot of tea was placed in front of them. "And anyway," her eyes following Mrs McCloud as she bustled out of the room, "you'll be working it off."

"I've married a harlot."

"I meant the walk you promised, although that could come later," she teased, rubbing the back of his hand before reaching for the milk jug. "It'll be nice to see Minou. Who'd you say was looking after him again?"

"Rexi, my spokesman." His eyes twinkling. "You know; the builder in the beanie? He had to rescue him from the cattery after the other cats started ganging up on him."

"Poor Minou, we'll have to make it up to him and to Rexi," she added, grinning across at him. "I know, we'll buy him a Tam O'Shanter and perhaps some shortbread."

"A Tam O what?"

"It's a tartan cap, my love," her voice trailing away as Mrs McCloud appeared back on the scene, weighed down with food.

"Here, let me help you with that." Pascal took the tray and waited while she placed their plates on the table.

"I'm afraid the sausages are a little overdone." She bustled. "I was listening to something on the radio."

"Oh, really?" He smiled across at Sarah, only half listening.

"It was wonderful." She continued, her eyes misty. "Someone's just donated eighty million to the Battersea Dog's Home."

"Oh really?" he repeated, his gaze locked on his wife's as he struggled not to laugh. "There are some generous people around."

"There are that. Well, I hope they receive their heart's desire, that's the truth. All them poor wee animals."

"Oh, I'm sure they will," he said, mouthing *I love you* across the table. "I'm sure they will."

The End

Dear Reader

Thank you for purchasing 'Englishwoman in Paris'. I hope you enjoyed reading about Lady Sarah and Pascal as much as I enjoyed writing about them.

'Englishwoman in Scotland,' the stand alone follow-up, is also available and I've added the start overleaf for your enjoyment.

Finally, thanks as always must go to my editor, Natasha Orme for helping me whip my manuscript into shape. It is edited to UK English though. Also thanks to my husband for helping me with the French.

If you'd like to get in touch I'm scribblerjb on Twitter. I also have a writer page over on Facebook called Jenny O'Brien Writes, in addition I blog at Jenny O'Brien writer, over on WordPress.

Best wishes

Jenny

Englishwoman

In

Scotland

Chapter One

'I'm going to kill myself!'
'Well do it quietly, darling. You know how much your father hates being disturbed before his second cup of coffee.'
'Mother...'
'There's no point in pleading. You've made your bed, and now you must lie in it. Your father is adamant, this time.'

The Countess of Nettlebridge beckoned to the butler with a carefully manicured hand. 'More toast please, Hodd and you might as well bring more coffee, I fear it's going to be a long morning,' her eyes now trained on the other end of the table where her husband was barely visible, behind The Telegraph.

'Yes, Madam.'
'Now, Titania, the announcement of your engagement to Viscount Brayely will be in The Times tomorrow and I think a June wedding. That will give us three months to sort out your trousseau. Harrods, of course, and then

there's the wedding dress. How do you feel about Alexander McQueen?'

'Mother, for the last time I am not going to marry some jumped up squirt of a viscount, especially one I've never met.'

'Why, of course, you have. You used to play together as children.' She sighed, picking up her lace edged handkerchief and patting it to her forehead. 'It has always been his mother's greatest wish. She was my bridesmaid, you know?'

'Yes, I do know. You've told me often enough.' She mumbled, staring across at her father who'd ditched The Telegraph in favour of The Guardian.

She'd always known about the close relationship between Lady Brayely and her mother but that didn't mean she had any intention of marrying her son, this boffin, or whatever he was. All Google had was a brief entry on Edinburgh University's webpage about his doctorate in physics, or was it chemistry? Whilst far from stupid, and a real asset at that quiz her mother had organised for homeless racehorses, she'd been far too busy at school with baking to worry about GCSE's or A Levels. With a path set out for her from childhood, one sweetened by the security net of millionaire parents, she'd done as little as possible. Watching Countdown was about as far as she went with regards to intellectual pursuits and yet, here they were setting her up for life with her worst nightmare. Her and this *Lord Brayely* might speak the same language but she wouldn't understand a word.

Leaning forward she placed a gentle hand on her mother's arm. 'Please, I promise I'll be good from now on. You can rely on me. You can't just sell me off the way granny sent the family silver to Sotheby's. You just can't.'

'Now, you're being ridiculous.' She replied, forcing a laugh. 'Family silver indeed. It was the ugliest epergne imaginable, and don't change the subject, Tansy. The only motive we have is a wish to see you settled with some nice young man.'

'Some nice young man who just so happens to be loaded and titled into the bargain. Just tell me this,' she added, lowering her voice. 'What's the going rate for an only daughter these days? Is it all about the money or is the title everything? At the very least I'd have thought I'd be good enough to snag a prince, or is it true that these days they really do prefer brunettes? Perhaps if I dye my hair black or even a striking red I might catch the eye of a count or even an earl. Yeah, I can live with that. Us blondes never seem to be anything other than blonde and it's about time I had a cut.' She said, smoothing her hand down the length of her hair. 'I've always fancied one of those pixie cuts, perhaps now is the time for a Titania make-over?'

'Now, don't go and do anything stupid. Everyone, as you very well know loves your hair. It's your trademark.'

'Well perhaps it's time for a rebranding. I wonder if I could sneak in a last minute appointment with Sebastian before this viscount arrives.'

She frowned, her thoughts now on why he'd agreed to such a crazy scheme.

'You haven't told me exactly why this lord wants to marry me? Why does he want to get married at all, and to someone he's never met?' She caught her mother's eye before adding, 'in like twenty years.' She tried to remember back to the visits she'd used to take with her mother, but all she could remember really was it was all very green and marshy. She remembered the marsh simply because she'd fallen in and nearly suffocated, or should that be drowned? Could you drown in mud? Not that the drowning part upset her half as much as the stink and the slime, and then there were the frogs. She'd always had a soft spot for frogs, ever since, but that was no reason to go and marry one.

'Not wants to, Titania. Is going to.'

'So? Is he poor or something? Is Daddy setting a huge dowry with at least ten thoroughbreds in addition to five thousand sheep...?'

'Don't be facetious, darling. The Brayelys' are loaded. They have a huge pile up in Scotland, although his mother, now she's a widow tends to spend her time between Berkley Square and the Riviera. It's so much easier to get decent staff in France.' She added quietly.

'Mother, you're not doing so badly. Hodd is a darling while Clemmy and Jessica are real treasures.'

'Treasure is the word. Do you know what the going rate for a butler is these days, darling?'

'You're avoiding my question.'

She sighed in exasperation at the thought of ever getting a straight answer out of her mother. Whilst she loved her dearly there was nothing and nobody more infuriating than her when she set her mind on something. Usually she'd just let it be; anything for a quiet life. If she did what her mother said, what time left was her own to do with as she wished. The fact she spent it messing in the kitchen was her business. Most mornings would find her wrapped in a large snowy white apron mixing, kneading and experimenting with a variety of results; some successful, some inedible. She had a tentative plan to write a recipe book on baking, but not just any old baking book with flans, quiches and cakes; a speciality bread book comparing and contrasting a variety of sourdough and traditional yeast breads from around the globe. The last time her mother had deigned to wander down to the kitchen on some pretext or other she'd been dismayed at the sight of the top shelf of the larder cupboard and all the containers filled to the brim with all the different starter kits but, apart from slamming the door shut on her way out she'd said little.

'What question, darling,' her mother asked, finally lifting her head from the Daily Mail, and the article on a six week bikini body. 'Do you think fifty is too old for a bikini?' She added, running a bejewelled hand over her rounded stomach.

'If I can be filmed topless there's hope for you yet, Mother.'

'Now you're being flippant, Tansy.' Her eyes still glued to the photo of Helen Mirren, resplendent in red. 'You don't realise what hurt you've caused.'

'Really?' Her face pale. 'And what about the hurt to me. Have you even considered what it's like been followed 24/7 by camera toting *paparazzi* shouting 'get your titties out, Titania?'

'Darling!'

'No.' She curled her hands around the arm of her chair as anger simmered just behind her eyes. She never lost her temper, perhaps it was time she started. Maybe it was time she did a lot more than lose her temper. Maybe it was time she put herself first, for once.

'Mother, do you know why this man wants to marry me? Do you know why anyone would want to marry someone with the whole of the British media on her tail; someone whose photograph has been stamped across every rag mag from Lands' End to John O Groats? You say he's rich and titled so it's not the money or the prestige. Is he ugly, is that it? It must be something?'

She watched her mother squirm when squirming wasn't really her thing, her eyes still carefully perusing Helen's many assets. 'He's not interested in women.'

'He's not interested in women,' her voice silk soft. 'What do you mean he's not interested in women? You mean he's…'

'Oh, he's not gay or anything. It's just he's not interested in anything unless it's in a petri dish.'

'In a petri dish?' She repeated, shaking her head. 'I don't understand. So he's not ugly.

He's weird. To be honest I'd have been happy with ugly. What man spends their life with a... What's a petri dish again?'

'Oh, you know, one of those agar plate thingy's. If you'd concentrated more in school and got yourself into university like your brothers we wouldn't be having this conversation.'

'Here we go again. Tell it to someone who's actually interested. So you're happy to sell me off to the only bidder, someone who's not interested in women...'

'I didn't say that.'

'Yes you did. In fact, those were your exact words.'

'Well, just think of it like this. As soon as you're pregnant with an heir he'll go back to his dishes and leave you alone.'

'Ah. The crux of the matter. So I'm to be mated like some cow in a field? I believe the term is artificially inseminated although there'll be nothing artificial about it. I'll have to put up with him slobbering all over me, buck naked until the job's done.' But her question would forever remain unanswered as her father's voice hollered from the other end of the table.

'Titania, are you still here? I thought I told you to stop badgering your mother and go to your room?' Her father boomed.

'But father...'

'No buts, my gal. No daughter of mine can expect to appear on the front page of the press with everything hanging out and expect to get away with it. You're just lucky the viscount is a man of letters and therefore probably unaware of your recent debacle.' He lowered the paper with a sharp rustle. 'As far as he is concerned you are still some sweet little thing in plaits and not some champagne swilling harpy with a large chest.'

'But they spiked my drinks, I know they did. One minute I was the designated driver and the next I knew I'd been bungled into the back of a taxi, minus my blouse and shoes.'

'A likely story.'

'But a true one all the same,' her voice now only a whisper.

'Titania, you have embarrassed your poor mother and I for the last time.' He paused, running his eyes up and down her slim form. 'Your explanations don't matter. Your opinions don't matter. You don't matter. You're actually getting long in the tooth for all this gallivanting. You should thank your dear mother for arranging it. Twenty-six is shelf material, you know.'

'Now hold on a minute,' her eyes flashing. 'What about Hamilton and Isaac? They're both older than me and I don't hear you nagging them to get married? In fact, I don't hear you nagging them at all.'

'Leave your brothers out of this. Men are different, as you very well know.'

'Oh yeah, here we go. Men get to do what they like, when they like, with whomever they like, while women are meant to suck it up with some pretentious git and get locked away to have babies. Bloody great!'

'Mind your language in front of your mother and there's no way out of this, Titania. I'm warning you. If you're not here to meet Lord Brayely for lunch, and in something other than denim, there will be hell to pay.' He shot a quick look across the table at his wife. 'You'll find we've temporarily cancelled all your credit cards just in case you're thinking of doing something stupid.'

'You've what! How dare you. That's my money...'

'No, that's your allowance I give you to amuse yourself with, until you get married. You're getting married and, therefore you'll be the viscount's responsibility. Any money you need ask your mother.' He added, picking up The Times, and turning to the back page.

Titania looked at both her parents with a little shake of her head, struggling to understand how her life, whilst not exactly spectacular had suddenly dissolved into a disaster zone. All she wanted, all she'd ever wanted was a quiet life, away from the limelight her parents were determined to thrust her into at every opportunity. If she had her way she'd open up a little café in the middle of some small country village and bake cakes all day. She'd have a counter on one side for breads and one of those fancy coffee machines that pumped out designer coffee at the push of a button. But the one and only time she'd tried to discuss it with them they'd laughed in her face at the thought of her, Lady Titania, the daughter of an earl, consorting with riff raff. So, instead, she spent her days consorting with a different type of riff raff; the type that had somehow engineered the elusive and quite frankly shy heiress to disgrace herself once and for all.

She made her way into the hall, smiling briefly at Hodd as he sorted out the post onto a silver platter, a frown on his forehead. But she didn't see the frown. She didn't see anything as she tried to figure out, for what seemed like the millionth time, what had happened on that fateful night.

It had started out like any other, which made the end all the more upsetting. She'd arranged to meet a couple of old school friends for a quiet drink but, before she knew it she'd woken up in the back of a black cab with cameras flashing through the windows as if she was somebody she wasn't. The press, all of them had her believe she'd been on a massive bender after a row with her boyfriend, some politician's son she'd never even heard of. If it hadn't been for the fatherly taxi driver, slinging his jacket in front of her, she'd never have been able to live it down. That crack of her father's about her chest was only partly true. There'd been skin, lots of skin but, by luck more than anything, she hadn't revealed much more than if she'd been lying on the beach. But that didn't matter to her father. Nothing mattered to her father more than the, so called, reputation of the Nettlebridges.

Printed in Great Britain
by Amazon